PREFACE

JULIET WINTERS CARPENTER

THIS FINE COLLECTION OF stories by revered author Miyamoto Teru, in Roger K. Thomas's expert rendering, deserves a wide readership. For decades Miyamoto has been a favorite of readers not only in the Kansai (Osaka-Kyoto-Kobe) region, where Miyamoto is from and which he writes about with verve, but throughout Japan. (Miyamoto regularly comes in at the top of an annual survey among Kyoto college students concerning both their "favorite" and "most recently read" author.) Following the acclaimed epistolary novel *Kinshu: Gold Brocade*, also translated by Thomas, international readers have been eagerly awaiting more of Miyamoto's delicately woven and emotionally nuanced, compelling works.

> "The juvenile image of myself went back down the alley that is myself."

> "I thought that that Mom's sudden derangement might be a transient phenomenon spurred by something or other, but that wasn't the case."

> "All the way to Wajima I talked to you, a dead man, as I looked out the window."

Miyamoto's characters are haunted by failures, by their inability to change events or themselves. They struggle to come to terms with life and death, and just to stay afloat. We feel a kinship with them as they quietly explore and sort out their fully believable emotions and situations. And, as the quotations above show, these stories beautifully capture the quiet, understated, moving tenor of Miyamoto's style.

Juliet Winters Carpenter
Kyoto, August 2011

Introduction

THE WRITER AND CULTURE critic Arlene Goldbard once noted that "our lives with all their miracles and wonders are merely a discontinuous string of incidents—until we create the narrative that gives them meaning."[1] Miyamoto Teru demonstrates consummate skill in creating such narratives with his sketches drawn from the working-class world of the Osaka-Kobe region in which he grew up, creating tales interspersed with vignettes informed by his own life experiences. And yet his approach, featuring no protagonist developed in a single work covering much of a character's life, differs markedly from what is generally termed "autobiographical fiction"—a genre calling to mind such works as Somerset Maugham's *Of Human Bondage* or James Joyce's *A Portrait of the Artist as a Young Man*. There is, nevertheless, much in Miyamoto's writing that mirrors his own personal history in various ways, and in order to appreciate how his authorial presence gives shape to his works and suggests a broad range of interpretive possibilities, it is useful to begin with a brief overview of his life and background.

Miyamoto Teru (given name: Miyamoto Masahito) was born in Kobe in 1947, a time when Japan was just beginning to recover from the ravages of the war. His father, Kumaichi—reflected in the characters of Shigetatsu in *River of Fireflies*

---

1 From an essay titled "The Story Revolution." See http://itp.nyu.edu/~mp51/collec-tive/goldbard-readingroom.pdf, last accessed August 16, 2011.

(*Hotarugawa* 1978) and Kumago in *Sea of Ceaseless Change*
(*Ruten no umi*, 1984)—was already fifty years old when finally blessed with a child, and in order to support his new
family attempted with varying success diverse ventures in the
emerging economy. As a young boy, Miyamoto grew up in a
milieu beautifully evoked in one of his earliest and best loved
works, *Muddy River* (*Doro no kawa*, 1977), in which Nobuo,
a boy whose parents run a small diner in a depressed area of
Osaka, befriends Kiichi, the son of a prostitute who plies her
trade in a ramshackle houseboat docked in a nearby river. In
a later essay, he recalls the spring of 1953 when he enrolled
in Osaka's Sonezaki Municipal Elementary School, nearly half
of whose pupils "were scions of families that ran small eateries or establishments of light entertainment." He remembers
walking to school with classmates through dark alleys where
they "horsed around and for no reason shouted curses as they
deftly jumped over the vomit here and there and the ground,
left by the previous night's drunkards."[2] Such scenes are hu-
morously reworked in "Strength" (*Chikara*, 1983).

In 1956, when Miyamoto was in his fourth year of elementary school, Kumaichi's business ventures took the family to
Toyama, an experience reflected in the reactions of the ado-
lescent Tatsuo to his new environment as seen in *River of Fireflies*. With the end of the Korean War and the ensuing reces-
sion, Kumaichi's business dealings began to face one setback
after another, and after only one year in Toyama, the family
relocated, first to Amagasaki in Hyogo Prefecture, and finally
to Osaka's Fukushima Ward. After several failed attempts at
business, Kumaichi's appearances at home became increasingly infrequent, and mother and son were often left desti-
tute. Perhaps serving as the background for his 1988 story
"The Stairs" (*Kaidan*), Miyamoto recalls in an essay that when
he was in his second year of middle school his "mother also
took to drinking during the day, and [he] would often come

---

2 From *Hatachi no hokage* (Tokyo: Kōdansha, 1983), pp. 18-19.

home from school to find her having drunk herself to sleep." One day she went to visit relatives, and still had not returned when Kumaichi showed up at 11:00 with the news that she had attempted suicide with an overdose of sleeping pills. As he turned to leave, his son threw an ashtray at him, breaking it on his back, whereupon Kumaichi said: "If your mother dies, then kill me. Kill me, and then you die too. . . . It's really simple for everything to fall apart."[3] His father returned later that night with the news that she had pulled through, and would be released from the hospital in a week.

Miyamoto recounts that he was so happy he cried. Unable to sleep, he shut himself in a closet and began reading a copy of Inoue Yasushi's (1907–1991) *Tale of Asunaro* (*Asunaro monogatari*) which a neighborhood friend had lent to him. He found himself "inexorably drawn into the world that unfolded before him. Possibly the event of [his] mother's attempted suicide had endowed [him] at that time with a sort of lucid sensitivity. Having [his] first encounter with the world of literature, [he] was so moved and intoxicated that it defied words."[4] That marked a turning point in his life; the boy who had previously avowed a strong antipathy to reading soon devoured every work of literature in his school's library, after which he went on to the public library and was never found without a book. He often took refuge from the unpleasant circumstances of his surroundings—his father's rage, or his mother's depression—by retreating into the closet and reading by the glow of a miniature light bulb. According to his own words: "Truly, my youth was spent together with pocket books."[5]

Far from losing his ardor, Miyamoto's love affair with literature only increased after he entered Kansai Ōgura High School, an all-boy's school in Osaka where he found his biology class to be a congenial place to indulge in reading works

---

3 From *Hatachi no hokage*, p. 58.

4 Ibid., p. 59.

5 Ibid., p. 61.

by such authors as Tolstoy, Mishima Yukio, Shimazaki Tōson, and Joseph Conrad, the last of these leaving an indelible mark on his thinking about the nature of literature. In 1968, when Miyamoto was a twenty-one year-old junior at Ōtemon Gakuin University, his father died, leaving debts from failed business dealings. Mother and son fled to a one-room apartment to evade creditors, and Miyamoto worked various part-time jobs in order to complete his degree, a situation reenacted by various characters in his works including Onodera in "A Tale of Tomatoes" (*Tomato no hanashi*, 1981). Due partly to too much time spent at various jobs ranging from bartending to road construction, his attendance at school became so sporadic that he only barely managed to graduate in 1970, whereupon he found employment as a copywriter with an advertising agency. Following marriage and the birth of his oldest son, Miyamoto resolved in 1974 at the age of twenty-seven to become a novelist. He quit his work at the declining advertising agency and, supporting his young family with odd jobs, wrote feverishly, finally gaining recognition when *Muddy River* won the thirteenth Dazai Osamu Prize in 1977. His productivity as a writer was temporarily slowed when he was diagnosed with tuberculosis in 1979 and hospitalized for a time, but following effective treatment he returned to writing at a feverish pitch.

Miyamoto's works lend themselves to cinematic interpretation, and several have been made into successful films, including *Muddy River* (Oguri Kōhei, 1981, Silver Prize at the Moscow International Film Festival), *Dotonbori River* (Fukasaku Kinji, 1982), *River of Fireflies* (Sugawa Eizō, 1987), *Oracion (Yūshun)*, (Sugita Shigemichi, 1988), and *The People of Dream Street* (Morisaki Azuma, 1989). Of the stories in the present collection, "Phantom Lights" was filmed in 1995 by the noted director Hirokazu Koreeda and released in the United States under the title *Maborosi*. It won the Golden Osella for Best Director at the 1995 Venice Film Festival.

Miyamoto certainly would not have become a writer without his passion for reading, and a desire to recast his personal experiences into a fictional mold perhaps also played no small role. But the diverse spectrum of writers who influenced him is also important to consider. He writes that as he was trying unsuccessfully to find his bearings as a writer while eking out an existence with unemployment insurance and his family's meager savings, he came across Yoshino Sei's (1899–1977) collection of essays *The God with the Runny Nose* (*Hana o tarashita kami*) in a bookshop and purchased it for no particular reason. Fascinated with the writing of this relatively unknown farmwife and mother of six, he ended up reading it over and over, and "whenever [he] would get stuck" in his own writing, he would "reread *The God with the Runny Nose*. And each time [he] would hit on something—'Ah, so *that's* it'—and then be able to proceed into [his] own world again with the manuscript paper before [him]." Six months later, he completed *River of Fireflies*, but felt that it still needed more work and set it aside while he began writing *Muddy River*. He writes that "both *Muddy River* and *River of Fireflies* could be said to have come into existence because of something [he] gained from *The God with the Runny Nose*."[6]

Defining Miyamoto's position in the world of Japanese letters is an exercise that has engaged few of his devotees; for the overwhelming majority of his extensive readership, it is sufficient to note that his works have an appeal that renders moot all questions of influence, artistic pedigrees, or relationship to the literary establishment. For Western readers who necessarily approach his works from outside their native cultural milieu, however, such questions will inevitably come to mind, and need to be addressed. Miyamoto's rise to literary prominence involved neither activity in a coterie nor the mentorship of an "establishment" (*bundan*) author; indeed, by the time he began writing, such connections no longer carried the

6 Ibid., pp. 132-133.

cachet they once did. But even in such an environment where relative independence was increasingly the norm, Miyamoto has always stood out as something of a maverick. Notwithstanding his voracious reading habits since his adolescence, in a 1977 essay he confessed: "Until just a few years ago, I was unaware that literature was divided into *belles-lettres* (*junbungaku*) and popular literature. I had always thought that, no matter which novel, if it's good, then it's good."[7] Indeed, his 1995 collection of essays on literary works that had impressed him profoundly—*A Boatload of Books* (*Hon o tsunda obune*)—includes works ranging from such native classics as Izumi Kyōka's (1873–1939) *The Holy Man of Mount Kōya* (*Kōya hijiri*) to popular works like Yamamoto Shūgorō's (1903–1967) *Tale of Aobeka* (*Aobeka monogatari*), and foreign works ranging from the "canonical" *The Flowers of Evil* (*Les Fleurs du mal*) by Charles Baudelaire (1821–1867) to *Johnny Got His Gun* by the American screenwriter and novelist Dalton Trumbo (1905–1976). And in a 1984 interview with the writer Nakagami Kenji (b. 1946), he describes his response when asked at a press conference how he differs from other writers: "If I were to say how I differ decisively from others, I think that it is that I, as a novelist, do not believe at all in ideation (*kannen*)."[8] In the same interview, he also argues that "in the final analysis, what human beings seek is hope, dreams, and happiness," but that "contemporary literature seems to go in the opposite direction." He recounts that as he lay in bed recuperating from tuberculosis, he felt a "desire to write about people who are trying to lift themselves up, who are struggling to live."[9]

Implicit in his opposition to "ideation"—or literature with an ideological bent—is both a criticism of much contemporary writing, and at the same time an assertion of his own independence from abstractions. But to say that he approaches writ-

---

7   Ibid., pp. 63-64.

8   From *Michi yuku hito-tachi to: taidanshū* (Tokyo: Bungei Shunjū, 1988), p. 110.

9   Ibid., p. 94.

ing with no "ideation" is not to say that he approaches it with no ideals. The kinds of things he seeks to achieve in writing are suggested in a 1980 essay entitled "A Tale Named Fate" (*Shukumei to iu na no monogatari*), which he opens with the following:

> There is a saying: people come with inherent disparities (*Hito wa, umarenagara ni sa ga tsuite iru*). It is an unremarkable saying, but it seems to suggest something extremely important. Speaking specifically of the world of fiction, it is not an exaggeration to say that it is because of these 'disparities' that an author is able to create a story.

He maintains that the aggregate of these inherent disparities—be they of status, of physical features, intelligence, or nationality—"can only be called fate," and that "many works of literature are records of defeat in the face of this fate." He notes that since literature is unable to alter the fundamental conditions that give rise to our disparities, much modern literature has simply taken to "fumbling about with the technique of fiction or with theory of method as it flees further and further from stories (*monogatari*) themselves." And yet, as human beings we are not able to transcend stories, and this brings literature to an impasse. He sees a resolution to this impasse in the words of Joseph Conrad (1857–1924), who wrote that a deserving and fortunate artist "may perchance attain to such clearness of sincerity that at last the presented vision . . . shall awaken in the hearts of the beholders that feeling of unavoidable solidarity; of the solidarity in mysterious origin, in toil, in joy, in hope, in uncertain fate, which binds men to each other and all mankind to the visible world." Miyamoto laments the fact so many writers "show no particular interest in such matters as 'joy,' 'hope,' or 'feelings of solidarity,'" and instead build their work "on a foundation of isolation and transitoriness." Literature has become jaded. And yet, "if there *is* anything new" in literature, "it is only to be found in those cases which demonstrate the testimonies and ways of how human beings burdened with the sadness, pain, and obstacles arising from fundamental 'disparities' managed to conquer the odds and turn things into a story of victory that suit their individuality." He takes Conrad's "feeling of solidarity" to be "another name for the power, will, and practices held in common by those who have driven out or shattered the merciless stories (*monogatari*) of mutually remonstrating fates in order to open the way to a better life and a better death."[10]

He is indifferent to whether his work is regarded as "belletristic" or popular. Since "storytelling" is something that cannot be transcended (as he sees many modern authors attempting to do), he aims rather to harness the process, including candid recognition of all our disparities which are the stuff of narration, and create a sense of "solidarity" through accounts of personal triumph and closure.

THE WORKS IN THE present volume develop a number of themes that are perennial in Miyamoto's fiction. All employ memory to develop the narrative simultaneously in layered frames of time, a technique at which Miyamoto is unusually adept. The mutual proximity—or even the identity—of life and death is a ubiquitous theme in his fiction. Relevant quotes are legion, but one of the most frequently cited is taken from the ruminations of the main character of his 1984 novel *A Spring Dream* (*Haru no yume*): "I wondered if the reason we know what happiness is might not be precisely because death is unquestionably lying in wait for us along the way. I came to feel that it was because there is death that human beings are able to live."[11] In the stories here, this theme is illustrated in Yumiko's talking to her late husband in "Phantom Lights," in the narrator's mother proclaiming her indifference to whether she lives or dies in "Eyebrow Pencil," and in the bicyclist who cannot make up his mind whether he wants to live or die in

---

10 From *Hatachi no hokage*, pp. 167-169. Conrad's words are taken from his own preface to his *The Nigger of the 'Narcissus'*.

11 *Haru no yume* (Tokyo: Bungei Shunjū, 1988), p. 113.

"The Lift." In other works the reader encounters characters who are plagued with a sense of having been left behind by the changing circumstances of their lives and the society around them, a theme that the critic Shibata Keiji has noted occurs repeatedly in Miyamoto's fiction.[12] In "Phantom Lights" Yumiko is left behind first by her grandmother's strange disappearance and then by her husband's inexplicable suicide, in both cases accompanied by the image of watching them walk away, her grandmother toward Shikoku and her late husband down the tracks, oblivious to the approaching train. Both were also seduced by "phantom lights," Yumiko's grandmother by the light of the late afternoon sun, and her late husband by the headlight of the approaching train. Yumiko herself is mesmerized by the illusory lights dancing on the waves.

Yumiko also attempts to determine what the "other meaning" of these "phantom lights" might be, first as she listens to her father-in-law explain the shimmer on the waves at the beginning of the story, and later as she contemplates the lights that seemed to rob her grandmother and her former husband of their will to live. What exactly was this "other meaning" that seems to be projected by these two retreating images? Getting beyond the illusion of the lights seems to be a parallel to solving this riddle. The critic Sakai Hideyuki argues that this question is more fully answered in Miyamoto's 1982 novel *Kinshu: Autumn Brocade* where Yasuaki describes in terms of an "other self" an experience as he lay dying:

> I was able to see myself on the verge of death. Another self was observing the self that was making a reckoning of the good and evil it had done, even as it was being subjected to excruciating pain . . . What was this other self? Could it have been my "life" itself, separated from my physical body?

Later, as Yasuaki contemplates his inevitable future death, he concludes: "I'll vanish from this world without trace. But my 'life,' cloaked in the mantle of good and evil with which I

12 See Shibata Keiji, *Oitekebori: Miyamoto Teru ron* (Tokyo: Kindai Bungeisha, 1996).

have been burdened, will live on."[13] In other words, "life" is karma, and the "other self" is the burden of karma one bears, and in narrating "how human beings burdened with the sadness, pain, and obstacles arising from fundamental 'disparities' managed to conquer the odds and turn things into a story of victory that suit their individuality," Miyamoto is suggesting the importance of confronting one's karma.

Both "Phantom Lights" and "Evening Cherry Blossoms" followed closely after the more autobiographical *River Trilogy* (*Muddy River*, *Firefly River*, and *Dōtonbori River*), and both represent an important stylistic shift, even using main characters of the opposite sex. In "Evening Cherry Blossoms," Ayako is likewise beset by a feeling of having been "left behind," both by her divorce and by her son's untimely death. This sense of having been passed by is accompanied by her advancing age—she is about to turn fifty—and by what she perceives as a loss of feminine essence. These feelings are juxtaposed with the image of scattering cherry blossoms. In the image of her uncomfortably tight obi, we see Ayako's inhibited sexuality, a view that is confirmed by various of her recollections: her dislike of being married even when she was fond of her husband, and her aversion to bathing with him. But judging from the uninhibited laughter coming from upstairs, the new bride enjoying her wedding night near the end of the story seems to have achieved something that had always eluded Ayako, and for a fleeting moment the scales fall from her eyes like the scattering of the blossoms she was viewing, and she catches a fleeting glimpse of the woman she might have been.[14]

In "Vengeance," Miyamoto's narrative craft takes the reader into the underworld of gangsters where a boss can control people's fortunes with a mere gesture. Its surprise ending suggests that the enduring pain of having suffered humiliation

---

13 See *Kinshu: Autumn Brocade* (New York: New Directions, 2005), pp. 100, 102-103. Sakai refers to this passage in his *Miyamoto Teru ron* (Tokyo: Kanrin Shobō, 1998), pp. 50-51.

14 Sakai expands on some of these points, p. 36.

at the hands of one holding absolute power might sometimes occupy a place in the psyche not far removed from sensual pleasure, a viewpoint that is bound to be controversial but one that is consonant with the mutual proximity of other seemingly irreconcilable opposites appearing throughout Miyamoto's works. But it is characteristic of Miyamoto's approach to writing that such potentially grim topics are not presented in a ponderous tone, but are rather often developed alongside humor. His narratives of personal triumph and hope are often set in situations involving death, illness, or loss, but what might be the stuff of tragedy in the hands of some writers turns into stepping stones for his characters to climb upward and onward.

NUMEROUS SMALL SACRIFICES ARE unavoidable in any translation, and it would ordinarily be unnecessary to belabor that fact by commenting about it. It is only fair, however, to inform readers of these stories that all dialogue appears in Kansai speech, and indeed the entire narratives of *Phantom Lights* and *The Lift* employ that regional variety of Japanese, which "feels" markedly different to native Japanese and to foreigners who have studied the language. The difference is in no way comparable to regional varieties of English, which tend to be regarded as "substandard"; on the contrary, the language of western Japan boasts a proud heritage all its own. As Edward G. Seidensticker conceded in his brilliant rendition of *The Makioka Sisters*, it is impossible to approximate the flavor of Kansai language in translation.

August 2011
Roger Thomas

A Tale of Tomatoes

トマトの話

At twelve o'clock on the dot, everyone set aside their various tasks, some opening their lunch boxes, others heading out to nearby cafés catering to office workers. For the past week, Onodera Kōzō had not had much appetite, and his lunches had been a fixed fare of udon noodles, delivered from the Kisaragitei noodle shop. When he called at 11:30 to place his order, he would ask colleagues in the Planning and Production Department, "While I'm at it, shall I place an order for anyone else? If it's only one item, they'll put it off to the very last, and I won't get it until after one."

Usually one or two others would say, "Well, in that case . . ." and order something like a rice bowl with beef or tempura. If a certain number of items could be ordered together, they would be delivered around noon as requested, but in some cases after only about ten minutes a delivery man would show up with his carrying box and boom, "Thanks for your order." At such times, those who had ordered would have to wait until noon, resigned to eat a cold meal.

Three months before there had been a reshuffling of personnel; the new director of the department was a man named Araki, under whom every aspect of office life was subjected to strict discipline. The advertising agency where Onodera worked was regarded as a company of medium standing, but in reality it was more like third-rate. Its attitude toward young employees in the department—including designers, illustrators, photographers, and copywriters, a group not adept at asserting themselves in dealing with the company organization—differed considerably from other leading agencies in its attempt to enforce conformity to established standards. In spite of that, the previous director had possessed a good understanding of such matters and would pretend not to notice if employees were a bit late or if they did not return from lunch until around three o'clock. He was of the opinion that as long as they got the work done, that was all that mattered; after all, designers and copywriters work better if given a degree of free rein.

But the new director, Araki, would sternly demand an explanation from anyone coming in even one minute late and remind those showing up in sweaters that the appropriate office attire was a jacket and necktie. As if perversely convinced that such discipline was all his job consisted of, he never eased up on his faultfinding, and in time even the members of our department—who, in all the company tended to conduct themselves as privileged exceptions—had completely assumed the veneer of white-collared workers, never daring to get up from their seats before noon rolled around and never failing to return to the production room by one.

Onodera slurped the udon noodles that had been sitting on his desk for nearly a half hour getting cold. Over a bowl of rice topped with tempura, Crow started up a conversation with another designer, Mitsuko, about their experiences with part-time work back in their student days. Crow's real name was Akagi Jun'ichi. His jet-black hair with a sheen like the wet feathers of a crow hung to his shoulders, and everything he wore—his jacket, his sports shirt, his necktie, his sweater—were all of the same raven hue whether in summer or in winter, so everyone just called him Crow. He possessed a quick wit behind his thick, rimless glasses, and even his minor quips bespoke a peculiar depth. Yet in terms of personality there was something almost pathologically careless about him. Especially when it came to money there was constant friction between him and his fellow designers.

Those who had been taken advantage of monetarily had harsh things to say about Crow and advised Onodera to have no serious dealings with him whatsoever. But Onodera liked Crow, who deliberately pretended foolishness and played the wag. He actually demonstrated a surprising sensitivity and intelligence that made him a good partner for Onodera's work as a copywriter. The conversation between Crow and Mitsuko piqued his interest, and, slurping his noodles, he sat down on a nearby chair. With a mixture of his characteristic facetiousness and comedy, Crow was telling about his work during a high school summer vacation for a company that sealed roofs against leaks, saying that he quit after a horrible three days he would never forget.

"Before pouring concrete onto the roof, we would spread layers of tar to prevent leaks. There were kerosene cans filled to the brim with boiling hot tar, and it was my job to carry them two at a time suspended from a bucket yoke. Since even the slightest contact could cause a serious burn, we wore thick rubber boots that came up to our thighs and long rubber gloves on both hands. You should try walking in that kind of getup carrying buckets of tar on top of a high-rise building under the blazing sun. After ten minutes of it, your head is already spinning. I don't know how many times the boss clobbered me with a bucket yoke because I spilled some tar. My contract was for ten days, but I chucked it after three. Those three days were hell."

Crow asked Onodera if some part-time work experience stood out in his memory. Only three of them were left in the production room: Crow, Mitsuko, and Onodera. Even Araki, who was usually sitting at his desk keeping vigilant watch over everyone's coming and going, was nowhere to be seen. Colored pencils of every hue, cutting knives, and cans of adhesive for pasting on the copy blocks were all lined up on the desk. Scattered about were the hundreds of sheets of positive film that the photographer had pretended to be hard at work examining only moments before.

When Onodera answered that he had held countless part-time jobs both in high school and in college, both Crow and Mitsuko pressed him to tell about the one that was most memorable. Onodera finished eating his noodles and looked at the clock. Forty minutes remained. He declined, saying that he didn't think he could finish telling about it in that much time, but the other two would not relent. Onodera lit a cigarette and inhaled the smoke deep into his chest. The last glint of the morning sun was magnified in his mind, and for some reason he felt that he had to talk. He began his account intending to wrap it up succinctly, but as he became absorbed in the various images projected in his brain, he was goaded by a strange excitement and continued talking with a most uncharacteristic smile.

My father died when I was a junior in college, leaving a lot of debts from his failed business. My mother and I evaded bill collectors by skipping out and moving to a little town on the outskirts of Osaka, where we rented an apartment with one six-mat room. Through the newspaper, my mother found an opening in the employee cafeteria of a business hotel within the Osaka city limits. I had resolved to quit college when my father died, but then reconsidered; since I had only two more years, I might somehow be able to graduate if I took on part-time work. One summer afternoon, I went to the Student Counseling Center near Ogimachi Park in Tenma. It was more like an employment security office and was packed with students seeking work. A friend had told me that I'd be sure to land some kind of job there.

Wanting to find something that would pay well even if a bit hard, my eyes immediately went to those parts of the listings indicating the daily wage. Jostling and pushing among people all about my age, I moved back and forth in front of the bulletin board. On slip number sixty-five was written "3,500 yen per day (with additional allowance for transportation)." Since the going rate for student work at the time was never more than 2,500 yen per day, I stared at slip number sixty-five thinking, "This is it!" The job was "traffic controller at a road construction site," and the hours were from eight in the evening until six o'clock the following day. It was scheduled for only ten days, not the lengthier three to six months I had hoped for, but during that week and a half I would make 35,000 yen. And when that job was finished, I could just find something else. With that in mind, I went to the clerk and conveyed my desire for job number sixty-five. Only five were needed, and four had already been hired, so I was the final applicant. After writing my name, address, and university affiliation on some documents, I was given a slip with the address of the job site, a simple map, and the name of the person in charge at the site, which was near the airport at Itami. It was in the Koya area of Itami City, the intersection between highway 71 and the national highway that goes to Takarazuka.

At a restaurant in the subterranean mall in Umeda, I ate ramen noodles, dumplings, and rice. Since it was an all-night job, I thought I had better eat a hearty meal before going. I took the Hankyū-Kobe line to Tsukaguchi, transferred there to the Itami line, and then from Itami station boarded the bus designated on the map and headed for the site. As I walked from the bus stop in the direction of Kobe, a large intersection came into view, countless blinking red lamps indicating that it was a construction zone. Two bulldozers were moving about. I asked one of the drivers where a certain Mr. Itō was, the one in charge.

"I saw him in the canteen."

With that, the driver—stripped to the waist and with a dirty towel as a headband—whirled the bulldozer around to the direction where I was standing and yelled, "Hey, get out of the way! If you don't watch out you'll get flattened!" Startled, I jumped aside to see another bulldozer pressing in on me, and I was treated to a string of invective such as I had never been subjected to before. It was not yet eight o'clock, but the work had already begun. Laborers in hardhats with pickaxes and shovels were collecting the scraps of asphalt that the bulldozer had spilled. A large searchlight trained on the worksite illuminated their grime- and dust-smeared faces and shirts.

On the top of a slope not far from the intersection stood the canteen, which consisted of two prefab buildings. The closer, oblong one was actually the dining area, and served as kitchen, cafeteria, and as a place where the workers could sleep. Tatami mats had been placed to the side of the cafeteria space, and several futons were left spread out. A thirty-ish, fat woman appeared to be busy in the kitchen, and I asked her where Itō was.

"In the office next door. You here for part-time work?" Her tone of voice was rough. When I answered in the affirmative, she said, "Did you eat before you came? If not, we have tons of rice balls here, so have as many as you like." She pointed to a large plastic container crammed with provisions the size and shape of softballs. Answering that I had already eaten, I hurried up the steep steps to the office next door. A man with a wild beard and an armband designating him as the site manager was on the phone shouting about something. Inside, four students who had, like me, been hired for part-time work were standing there looking quite helpless. I handed the documents I had received at the Student Counseling Center to a young man in work clothes. Apparently he was Itō. He shouted to the man with the wild beard, "Hey, all five are here now." The site manager was short but had a stocky build of about ninety kilograms. After hanging up the phone, he approached us with a large diagram in one hand.

"This construction project will repair the asphalt right in the middle of the intersection. Your job will be to stop cars in all directions. The police have shut down the traffic lights, so in effect you'll be traffic signals. Until morning, it will be one-way traffic through the intersection. You'll have to stop either the east and west or the north and south cars, allowing only one-way traffic to pass through."

With perspiration dripping off his double chin, the site manager explained the job in a surprisingly calm tone. Since I had found his face so menacing, I felt a bit relieved, and cast a glance at the four other students whose names I didn't know. All of them were staring at the diagram with tense expressions.

"If your timing is even a little off, it can cause a major traffic jam, and then you can't get it under control again." Drawing a map of the site on a blackboard, the manager assigned us to our respective posts and explained how to direct traffic. First, you stop traffic in all directions. Next, you take care of cars that are headed east, at which time the person at that post has to signal to everyone asking if the way is clear by swinging both arms in big circles using the red flashlights. The signal that it's okay is made by swinging one flashlight left and right. Until you get that confirmation, you should never let any cars go. Once you've taken care of a certain number of eastbound cars, next you let westbound traffic pass through, observing the same points. Then when you're finished with the east-west traffic, you take care of the north-south cars." The manager went over the signals again and again, and had each of us rehearse them in turn.

"The most important one is the guy who stands in the middle of this intersection." That was my post. The manager said to me, "Bulldozers will be moving around in the intersection, and dump trucks will be coming and going one after another, so you need to use caution in directing the cars. Today, we'll be replacing the asphalt on the south half of the west side of the intersection, and so you'll have to divert all the east-west traffic through the north side. The same points hold true for the north-south traffic. If you mess up in directing them, the cars will run into dump trucks, and . . ."

Having said that much, he was silent for a while, then finally added with an air of gravity, "And that's not all: You, too, could be flattened by a dump truck or a bulldozer."

"Will I be standing in the intersection all ten days?" I asked timidly.

The manager thought for a while, and then perhaps concluding that it was the most dangerous and exhausting post, said, "Let's rotate positions on a daily basis. At any rate, you'll get the hang of it tonight, and then it'll be easier after tomorrow. But if you're standing in the middle of the intersection, you can't let your mind wander. Two or three guys have been killed or seriously injured through inattention."

I began to think that maybe I wanted to quit if the work was that dangerous. As I was just about to say so, a worker came rushing in, "Sir, we're ready to start!" We took the flashlights that had been provided for us, put on our hardhats, and were sent running to the site. After the manager and Itō yelled out commands for us to take our posts, the policeman who had arrived to turn off the traffic signals waved his arm. There was no escaping now. The traffic signal was turned off, and vehicles in all directions were halted by the orders of students doing part-time work. Just then, the bed of a dump truck raised and deposited an enormous pile of hot asphalt right next to me.

"Hey, d'ya wanna get killed?" the manager shouted at the top of his lungs. The eastbound traffic had begun to pass through, and so, dodging bulldozers and dump trucks and hissing hot mounds of asphalt, I furiously waved the red guide lights in both hands, sending the passing cars one after another in an easterly direction. Then at a different signal the westbound cars began to move, and when they had finished passing through, next the southbound, and so forth. Long lines of halted traffic began to flow at the direction of the guide lights waved about by mere students doing part-time work. Dodging bulldozers and the roughneck driving of huge dump trucks, I ran back and forth, continually waving the flashlights to show endless lines of vehicles the path through the chaos. Before an hour had passed, the smell of the asphalt and the exhaust fumes of the passing cars were making my throat sore. I seriously thought I might die if I kept at this for ten days. Streams of perspiration flowed from under my hardhat into my eyes, which I wiped with the backs of my hands. But the volume of perspiration only increased, and so I took off the hardhat and tossed it to the side of the road. At that, Itō came running up with a furious look on his face.

"If you don't keep your hardhat on, you'll end up with a serious head injury. Trucks will be leaving with huge loads of the old asphalt, and if any of that falls and hits your head, it'll be curtains!"

I hurriedly picked up my hardhat and fastened it on my head, then asked if I could go get the towel I had left in the office. Seeing my perspiration, Itō clicked his tongue and agreed. While I was away, he would direct traffic in my stead. I ran to the canteen and asked the fat woman for some water.

"There's chilled barley tea over there that'd be better than water," she said, taking out a teacup with a chipped rim and pouring from a large teapot. Gulping down three cups of barley tea one after another, I went to the office, got my towel, and returned to the dining area, where I drank three more cups of tea while wiping off the perspiration.

"Would you like some barley tea, too?" the woman asked. She was facing the oblong tatami room where the quilts had been left spread out and which I had thought was empty. As I wiped my face, I cast a glance toward the farthest part of the canteen where the lights had been extinguished. Someone was lying on a futon in the corner. He didn't respond but just rolled over and groaned slightly.

"Take this tea over to him." I took off my shoes and carried the cup to the dark corner, where an emaciated middle-aged man was sprawled out on a futon. When I placed the cup by his pillow, he opened his eyes and looked at me for a moment, then closed them without saying a word, ignoring the tea. As I was about to move away, he said something.

"Huh? What was that?" I asked.

"I want some tomatoes." the man said in an indistinct voice.

"Tomatoes?" I relayed the man's request to the woman in the kitchen.

"You think we'd have anything like tomatoes here now? I'll buy some for you tomorrow," the woman shouted to the man in the dark recess. I stuffed the towel into my back pocket and rushed back to my post.

After midnight, the traffic finally decreased. By then the students had the knack of the work down, so almost no trouble occurred from miscommunication with signals. After about three a.m. it cooled down a bit, and in any direction there were never more than about seven or eight vehicles waiting for our signals. But lots of dump trucks were still moving in and out one after another, the same as before. They'd enter the site with ferocious speed and leave the same way. Heavy machinery for digging up the old asphalt and the bulldozers collecting the rubble were moving about under blazing floodlights. The four other students were able to sit on the side of the road and rest while the traffic was stopped, but being out in the middle of the intersection, I couldn't let my attention wander even for a moment. My legs felt leaden and the arches of my feet began to ache with a burning sensation. From the sloping path in front of the canteen the manager shouted something to me. Between the noise of the rock drills and the bulldozers, I couldn't make out a word he was saying. Then a worker came up to me and yelled into my ear that the manager was calling me, and that he'd fill in for me. I went to the manager, who motioned for me to go inside where he pointed to a chair.

"Sit down. The guys at the other posts can rest now and then, but you're left standing until morning. Take it easy here for a while." Then he pulled a cigarette out of his shirt pocket. "You smoke?" I accepted the manager's offer, and lit up. "It's tough work, but if you stick it out and don't quit, we'll pay you a little extra at the end."

The manager smoked too as he sipped his chilled barley tea. I peered into the back of the canteen and asked, "Is that guy sick?"

"The day before yesterday some recruiter for day laborers brought him by. He was fine then, but last night he collapsed in the middle of the road. Just when we were thinking of calling a doctor, he came to and said he'd be able to work again if he could only rest a day or two. That's why he's in bed. If he doesn't work he doesn't get paid, so it doesn't really matter as far as we're concerned, but if he's sick, he needs to see a doctor."

He added that the company couldn't pay for medical treatment for day laborers. And since he didn't belong to any company or organization, workmen's compensation wouldn't apply in his case. A lot of them don't give their real names, or conceal their ages and birthplace, and that makes it even more difficult to take care of them. The manager looked at his watch and returned to the site, reminding me to go back to my post in fifteen minutes. Several large flies were buzzing around me annoyingly, and the interior of the canteen was stifling with the stench of food and the lingering heat. I poured some barley tea into a cup and went to the man's side. This time he heard my footsteps and watched me approach with his eyes wide open.

"Won't you have some tea? You must get thirsty in this room." Without rising, the man nodded and thanked me in a weak voice, but made no move to drink the tea.

"Shouldn't you go see a doctor?" The man responded to my suggestion with a smile but just closed his eyes without saying a word. It was dark, and I couldn't see his face clearly, but I sensed that his condition was very serious. About five days before my father died, I had a premonition that he would only last another five or six days. In the gaunt frame of the man lying on the futon there was a shadow peculiar to the sick facing their final hours.

"I'd like some tomatoes. Won't you buy some for me?" The man spoke with his eyes closed. It occurred to me that he must be from Kyushu. One of my college friends from Kyushu had a similar accent.

"The lady in the kitchen said she'd get some for you tomorrow."

"She just says that. I asked her yesterday too, but she just said she forgot and didn't buy any."

"Well then, I'll get some and bring them tomorrow."

With that, I returned to the site. The time passed quickly until six o'clock. The sky was bright before five; by six, the sun was already out and it was a bit hot. At six on the dot, the work ended and the traffic lights came on. We dragged our exhausted bodies back to the canteen. On the way, we students talked to each other for the first time.

"These next nine days are going to be hell," a student named Ōnishi muttered, addressing no one in particular.

"Then the guy who stands in the middle of the intersection is right in the center of hell," I said.

The short one, Nakatani, who was scheduled to be in the middle the following night, remarked, "It scared the hell out of me to watch you run around out there. You probably didn't notice it, but several times you were almost hit from behind by a dump truck." Since the construction was scheduled for ten days, I'd be out in the middle one more time.

Breakfast for dozens of people was ready in the canteen. After a night's work I had no appetite, but I forced down some tofu, miso soup containing slices of potato, and rice with egg. Then I went to the lavatory that had been set up in front and washed my face. A young guy, probably a day laborer, told me there was a makeshift shower. Behind a barrack was an enclosure made out of tinplate with a hose suspended into it. After shedding all my clothes, I turned the spigot and let the water wash the perspiration off my body. But my underwear, trousers, and shirt were still full of sweat and dust, and when I put them back on I felt grimier than before. After finishing their meal, the laborers slept like logs until evening in the inner room of the canteen, where there was neither air conditioning nor even a fan.

We took the bus to the Hankyū Itami Station. From there it was nearly another two hours to my home. I was so exhausted that I wondered if I shouldn't just sleep on a bench in the station until evening. After saying good-bye to the others at Umeda, I managed to drag myself onto a car on the Osaka Loop Line and changed to the Katamachi Line at Kyōbashi station. Collapsing into the soiled seat of the ancient train car, I made a point of staring out the window at the blindingly bright sky so as not to fall asleep. It was about a half-hour ride to the station where I got off, and after making the long walk from there to our apartment, it was just before ten when I finally arrived. Entering the room I found that my mother had scrawled a note in pencil and left it on the small dining table. She told me to be sure to get plenty of sleep when I got home and to eat a good dinner before setting out for work that evening. I opened the window, changed into my pajamas, collapsed onto the futon and fell asleep with the fan on. It was five in the evening when I awoke. After using a damp towel to wipe down my still exhausted and heavy body, I got dressed and left the apartment. At the same Chinese restaurant in the subterranean mall at Umeda, I consumed the same food as the day before, and then boarded the Hankyū train.

Near Itami Station, I bought five tomatoes. As soon as I arrived at the site, I went to the man lying in bed in the back room of the canteen. I set the tomatoes by his pillow and was about to say something when I perceived the quiet breathing of his sleep.

The work that night was far easier. I stood directing vehicles in the road extending north from the intersection. The other students had also gotten the hang of the job, and it went pretty much without a hitch. As we became relaxed around each other, a feeling of camaraderie grew among us, and we even took turns spelling the one assigned to the middle of the intersection in order to let him rest once every hour. Or one of us would steal into the canteen and, while the cook had dozed off, pilfer some rice balls to share with everyone, or secretly buy some canned drinks for the others. Several days went by like that.

It was just two days before the completion of the project. As I was in the canteen drinking barley tea as usual, the bedridden man staggered to his feet and called to me. He looked as if he could not stand without holding on to something, so I supported his arm and took him back to his futon, where I gently laid him back down. From under his pillow, the man took an envelope containing a letter and asked me if I would post it after work the next day. I thought it a simple request and, promising to do so, stuffed it in my back pocket. I glanced at the side of his pillow and noticed that all five tomatoes were still in the bag, the same five I had bought six days before. Puzzled, I asked, "You didn't eat the tomatoes?"

The man nodded weakly and, with a faint smile, took one of the tomatoes out of the bag, placed it momentously on his chest, and stroked it with both hands.

"If you just leave them there, they'll rot." They were already overripe and beginning to lose shape. He didn't respond but, cradling the tomato on his chest, just reminded me to be sure to post the letter. I repeated my promise as I stood up. After taking a few steps, I glanced back and saw a wistful look in his eyes, which were full of tears as he wrapped both hands firmly around the tomato. I realized that he hadn't had me buy the tomatoes out of a desire to eat them. But then why did he want them so badly? I went back and advised him to see a doctor as soon as possible.

"I don't have much longer," the man said as he turned away.

I returned to the kitchen where I drank some barley tea. I cinched the strap of my hardhat and took the letter out of my back pocket to look at it. In a childishly awkward hand written with a ballpoint pen it had been addressed to a Ms. Kawamura Setsu in Kagoshima Prefecture. The sender's address was missing; only his name appeared: Emi Hiroshi. Only then did I know what his real name was. The site manager bellowed at me to get back to my post right away, so I stuffed the letter back into my pocket and rushed back to the intersection. That day it was my turn to stand in the middle of the intersection. Unlike the first day, there were fewer dump trucks going in and out, and only one bulldozer was moving about. The old surface had all been dug up and there remained only the task of laying down new asphalt. The work proceeded smoothly. The air had usually been still, but that night a cool westerly breeze was blowing, and I didn't even perspire much.

It must have been past two a.m. when I heard the siren of an ambulance approaching from the distance. We had been instructed in such cases to stop traffic in all directions and let the ambulance pass, and so we gave the appropriate signal. When the ambulance reached the middle of the intersection, it stopped. The cook waved to it from the entrance to the canteen, and Itō and the site manager came rushing out.

"He still has a pulse," the manager said to the ambulance crew, and then went back inside. They took out a stretcher and headed for the building. It had not occurred to us that this construction site might be the destination of the approaching ambulance, and the students raced from their respective posts to where I was to discuss what to do about the halted traffic. Except for the cook, the only person in the canteen was the guy named Emi; there could be no doubt that something had happened to him. I told the four others that someone had fallen ill and that the only thing we could do was to apologize to the driver of each vehicle for the delay and explain that they would need to wait until the ambulance left. The four dispersed all at once and walked about explaining the situation to every head poked out of a window venting displeasure, asking, "What's going on?" or "Let us go already!"

The stretcher bearing Emi was loaded into the ambulance, and the site manager got in to accompany him. They set out to the north, and as soon as the halted traffic began moving again, I handed my flashlights to a nearby worker saying that I would be right back. I rushed inside where the corpulent cook was standing, staring blankly at the place where the man had been lying. I turned on the light in the room where the futon had been spread out for so long. The area was awash in blood in which were lying five rotting tomatoes.

"What happened? Hey, what happened to that guy?" I asked, grabbing the shoulder of the cook, who was backing away in horror.

"I don't know. Just as I was making rice balls I heard groaning. When I turned on the light and looked in the back, he was vomiting blood like a whale spouting."

The tomatoes in the blood spreading over the tatami looked like blood clots, as if the man had spit them up. I had to remind myself that they were indeed tomatoes. I returned to my post in the intersection, thanked the man who had stood in for me, and got back to work. I recalled the site manager saying Emi still had a pulse and thought that he was sure to die. Perhaps he was already dead. As I was directing the passing cars with practiced gestures, his words and his attempt to hide his tears came to mind: "I don't have that much longer." He must have realized that the end was near.

Just then, someone tapped me on the shoulder. I turned around to see Itō standing there. "I'll take over here. Why don't you go to the canteen and help out there." He said they were burning the blood-soaked futon and pulling up some of the tatami mats to wash them. The cook was too spooked by the whole thing and refused to enter the room, so two or three workers and I were asked to burn the futon, take up the tatami mats, and hose the blood off them. As I was about to head to the canteen to do as instructed, Itō added, "He died immediately after arriving at the hospital."

"He died?"

Itō nodded silently then motioned with his chin for me to go right away. Two trucks entered the intersection and began to dump steaming fresh asphalt to pave over the last remaining area.

We poured lamp oil on the futon and ignited it. Then we took up the tatami mats, carried them out to the vacant lot in front of the canteen and, using a hose and scrub brushes, washed off all the gore that was beginning to harden and blacken. While we were engaged in that task, the manager returned from the hospital.

"They told me to come by tomorrow morning and pick up the remains." Muttering to no one in particular, he went to the room where the man had been lying and began collecting his belongings, which consisted only of a simple sewing kit stuffed into a small soap box, several changes of yellowing underwear, a passbook for a savings account with a balance of only eighty-six yen, and his seal. With those items in his hands, the manager stood next to me as I was washing the tatami. He stared at the characters on the seal.

"He said his name was Egawa, but his seal says Emi," he said, clicking his tongue. "Even if I retrieve his remains, I have no idea where his family is or where he's from."

Intending to mention the letter Emi had entrusted to me, I set the hose down and reached into my back pocket. I gasped as I groped around. It wasn't there. I felt the inside of all my trouser pockets, even the small shirt pocket over my breast. The letter had fallen out someplace. I searched everywhere I had been, including the intersection that had been my post that day, but with no success. I ran back to the canteen at full speed and asked the cook if a letter had been found. Answering in the negative, she continued to make rice balls with a stiff expression such as I had never seen. Seeing how panic-stricken I was as I kept going back and forth over the same ground, the manager asked what was wrong. I checked the words that nearly came out—"a letter from Emi"—and just said, "I've lost a letter."

"A letter? An important one?"

"Yes." I was on the verge of tears. The characters for "Ms. Kawamura Setsu," awkwardly written with a ballpoint pen, came to my mind. I took off running again, and when I got back to the place in the intersection where I had been standing not long before, I ran about scanning the ground, all the time being yelled at by bulldozer drivers. The wide, shallow hole that until not long before had been littered with excavated rubble was now neatly filled in with fresh, pitch-black asphalt onto which workers were sprinkling water. With a feeling of horror, I stared at the road and its new asphalt. The letter must have fallen out of my pocket here. I couldn't think of any other possibility. It had been buried forever under the hot asphalt. Surely that was the case. Half-sobbing, I shouted at a bulldozer driver, "Please take up this asphalt. There's a letter underneath it."

The driver shut off the engine and stared at me blankly. I clambered up to the driver's seat and repeated my plea, the tears finally spilling over. The driver exchanged glances with Itō.

"Are you some kind of idiot? You're asking me to take up this asphalt? It's seven square meters. Just to redo it would take a hundred times your wages!"

"But I lost a very important letter here. I'm sure it's under this." Grabbing his thick muscular arm I pleaded frantically.

"Hey, Itō, this guy's lost his marbles." The driver lightly shook his arm free from my grasp and, starting up the engine, refused to give any more ear to my appeals.

"What's going on here?" Hearing the commotion, the manager came up, his hefty body swinging with each step. Itō explained the situation to him as I stood there rubbing myself to calm my trembling. The manager rapped my hardhat with his slide rule and said, "You really dropped it here?"

"Yes."

"You'd better just forget about it and stop spouting such idiocies as 'tear up the asphalt.' What a blockhead!" Then he said to Itō, "Emi Hiroshi seems to be his real name. That's what appears in his savings passbook."

"What kind of ailment was it?" Itō asked.

"They said a blood vessel in his esophagus burst. It seems that's what happens eventually when the liver's no good anymore."

"So, his liver was bad?"

"The doctor said he was in the final stage of cirrhosis, and that in any case he wouldn't have lasted much longer."

The morning the construction was completed, all of the workers, student part-timers, and employees of the construction firm gathered in the canteen to toast the occasion with beer. Just as the manager had promised, in addition to our ten-day wages he added a gratuity of ten thousand yen for each of us, along with thanks.

"Thanks for your hard work. You can go home now. All that remains to be done here is to dismantle the canteen."

With that, he drained the beer in his paper cup and hurried up the stairs to his office. The students I had worked with those ten days invited me to go along to Itami Station, but I stayed behind to make one more search, checking the grass by the canteen and the edge of the neatly paved intersection to see if, by some remote chance, the letter might be lying somewhere. The midsummer sun was beating down on my exhausted body.

Knowing that his end was near, Emi Hiroshi had mustered his last reserve of strength and written a letter to a woman named Kawamura Setsu. I don't know what kind of relationship they had, but what had been jotted down in those awkward characters was no doubt very important to them. I tried to recall the parts of the address other than Kagoshima Prefecture, but absolutely nothing remained in my memory. And even if I had been able to remember, how could I possibly explain to Kawamura Setsu about the letter? Long after my coworkers had left, I was still wandering around the construction site, staring alternately at the ground and the blazing morning sun.

Even after graduating from college and starting work at this advertising agency, I still have moments when, for some reason, I call to mind the figure of that man squeezing the tomato with both hands, his eyes welling up with tears. When I'm making arrangements with a sponsor, it will suddenly rise up in my mind. When I sit down in the last train at night looking at my drunken face reflected in the window, the image of those five rotting tomatoes lying in a pool of blood will flash before my eyes. At those times, the characters for "Kagoshima Prefecture" and "Ms. Kawamura Setsu" inevitably rise like specters from somewhere deep within me. Then, as if it had been my own illness, I become lost in thought wondering what the tomatoes could possibly have meant to him and what things of importance were written in that letter. I'm convinced that even now that letter lies buried beneath the asphalt in a major intersection in Koya at Itami. It isn't that I am repelled by the image of the five rotting tomatoes that looked like blood clots, I haven't eaten so much as a single slice of tomato since then.

Evening Cherry Blossoms

夜桜

Teased by spring breezes, Ayako trudged up the steep road leading from the Hankyū Mikage Station through a quiet residential area. The sunny path was carpeted with petals falling from cherry trees in full bloom.

Her obi was too tight, causing discomfort in the pit of her stomach. Before long she would turn fifty. Twenty years had passed since she had divorced her husband, and soon it would be a year since her only son, Shūichi, had died in an accident.

As she paused in her ascent of the steep road and looked back, the sea at Kobe came into view, glittering through the spring haze like a sheet of silver. Even when she was in good spirits, gazing at the sea from this vantage had never elicited a feeling of happiness. Whenever she spotted large passenger ferries under tow or cargo ships, a strange sadness would well up within her, and she would stand transfixed for a long time gazing out over the distant waters. Ayako's house was about a hundred meters farther up the road, sandwiched between a bank president's mansion and the Western-style house of a German trader. It was a two-story cypress wood house surrounded by a spacious garden with tall shrubbery. Ayako and her husband had gotten it for a song two years after their marriage from a speculator who had fallen on hard times.

To the left, the Rokkō Mountains came into view. The cars ascending up the toll road seemed pea-sized as they disappeared into the greenery. Aside from the occasional shouts of children playing, not a single sound could be heard on the sloping road. Ayako began walking again. The cherry blossoms blowing in the wind annoyed her. She recognized a female college student coming toward her, who in passing said with a smile, "It seems you have a visitor."

Out of breath from hurrying and with perspiration beading on her neck and back, Ayako turned right from the street to find Yamaoka Yūzō, her ex-husband, standing in front of the house.

"Sorry to drop by unannounced. I had some business at a department store in Umeda, and . . ."

At Shūichi's funeral the year before, she had for the first time in twenty years seen Yūzō, who had come by later to help with arrangements for the memorial services on the thirty-fifth and forty-ninth days. He was three years older than Ayako and ran a shipping company in Kobe.

"What's this?" Yūzō asked, pointing at the gatepost. On her way out Ayako had put up a poster that said: "Room to let. Student only. Guarantor required."

"Well, the upstairs is empty, and . . ."

"Are you hard up for money?" Yūzō asked with a frown. When Ayako did not respond, he continued with a stern glare, "That's not necessary. All you have to do is tell me."

"That's not it at all. It's dangerous for a woman to live alone, and besides I thought it might be a welcome diversion to have someone else in the house."

"There are so many weirdos among students these days that taking one in is probably more dangerous."

"Oh, really?"

Entering the house, Ayako showed Yūzō into the eight-mat room facing the garden. Originally it had been the guest room, but since Shūichi's death Ayako had occupied it. When she opened the large glass doors to the veranda, Yūzō stood beside her looking out at the cherry trees in the garden.

"They're in full bloom."

"They seem to be about five days earlier this year than last."

Shuichi had died on the tenth of April, when the cherry trees in the garden were at their most beautiful.

"The blossoms here are especially nice."

It was no doubt just as Yūzō said: Compared to the cherries at other residences, these really stood out, both for their color and for the profusion of their blossoms. Three huge trees towered over the middle of the spacious garden, their branches intertwined. They had been there when Yūzō's father bought the place from the speculator after the war.

"Even when the cherries bloom at my place, they look pathetic."

Ayako was anxious to undo her obi and change into something more comfortable, but with Yūzō there she felt rather constrained. Relatives from her side of the family had been present on the day of the funeral and also during the services for the forty-ninth day, so it was the first time in twenty years she had been alone with her former husband.

Sitting cross-legged on the cushion Ayako put out for him, Yūzō said, "About the first anniversary services for Shūichi, I'll take care of everything, so you don't need to worry." Yūzō quickly corrected himself when he was about to address her with the familiar "Aya."

Looking at his bristly, almost completely white hair, Ayako became aware that everything she had repressed those twenty years was gradually building up within her. From where she sat on the tatami, she fixed her eyes on the cherry blossoms in the garden. As if spilling from their crowded cage of branches, petals fell to the ground along with the spring sunlight.

"Is the German guy next door still alive?"

"Yes. I hear he'll turn eighty this year, but he's in good health. His youngest grandson married a Japanese woman. They say that didn't go over well with his grandpa, and it turned into quite a row."

"Well, after coming to another country to become lord of his own kingdom and castle, that's a bit bigoted, don't you think?"

"Is your work going well?" Ayako asked Yūzō.

"Not really, but business is bad everywhere, so there isn't much I can do about it. I'm always at the office until ten or so."

"I'm sure you find time, though, to dally with young women," Ayako added with a sarcastic smile.

"You think I still have the energy for that sort of thing?" Yūzō cast a dejected glance at his former wife.

"If I'd known that Shūichi would die before me, I'd never have divorced you. I made a mistake that can't be undone."

Her words bore a similarity to those of Yūzō's proposal of marriage more than two decades earlier. Twenty-five at the time, he had whispered the words passionately at a membership-only restaurant in Kobe's Kitano district, a high-class place run by a foreigner, which was unusual then.

"If I hadn't suddenly been drafted, I'd have proposed to you sooner. Even if I'd known that I was going to die, I'd still have made you mine. Not having proposed sooner was a mistake that can't be undone. I've always thought so." It struck Ayako as amusing when those exact words emerged vividly from her memory. The Korean War had begun, and the shipping business run by Yūzō's father was making money hand over fist. Yūzō had inherited his late father's business two years after the divorce.

"I've never had a chance to tell you before now, but my dad worried about you. Right up until he died he used to say it would be a load off his chest if you found a good man and remarried."

She recalled her father-in-law's silver hair and gaunt frame as he prostrated himself at the entrance to this house and apologized to Ayako in an attempt to dissuade her from seeking a divorce. Through sobs, she had screamed "No!" like a fretful child. "I could put up with it if I hadn't seen it with my own eyes. But I did see it, right there before me, another woman in Yūzō's arms, and now there's no way I'll stay with him!"

It occurred to Ayako that what "couldn't be undone" were those words she had uttered. Having finally married after a protracted courtship, Yūzō and Ayako parted after a mere three years together. It was her father-in-law who saw to it that she got custody of one-year-old Shūichi and who gave her this house in Mikage. Although she received monthly child-support payments, Ayako went to work when Shūichi turned three. An uncle of hers ran an imported goods shop in Rokkōguchi. At first, she only helped out with simple office chores, but eventually she learned how to maintain inventory and wait on customers, and after three years she was managing the place. She had no desire to own the shop, but continued to work there until Shūichi's death. Several people had suggested remarriage, but that prospect never sparked her interest, an important reason being that she had her own house and was comfortable with her circumstances. But more than anything else it was because she could never forget her ex-husband. He had been a privileged young man unacquainted with hardship, but sometimes it occurred to her that she, too, had been a pampered young miss. When she had gotten news of Yūzō's remarriage, she had walked in a daze back and forth for hours along the banks of the Ishiya River, leading Shūichi by the hand. That was all in the distant past.

As she poured hot water into the teapot, Ayako glanced at Yūzō's spring three-piece suit. It was well-tailored, gray with a slight cast of blue.

"To show such youthful taste in a suit, you must still have ambitions."

"Give me a break. My oldest daughter is already thinking of getting married."

Yūzō crawled on all fours across the tatami and with both hands picked up a celadon jar displayed in the alcove.

"This really brings back memories."

Her father-in-law, who had treasured it, had given it to Ay-ako when she divorced Yūzō. Her father-in-law's big, gentle eyes appeared in her mind, and she surprised herself by saying, "Back then I should have said, 'I'll let it go this once, but never, ever cheat on me again.' Then Shūichi wouldn't have died." She suddenly burst into tears. Pressing the jar to his chest, Yūzō looked at her without saying a word.

"I was a spoiled young miss, and you were a spoiled young master."

Given over to weeping, Ayako was overcome with an unbearable feeling of despair. A sadness as if she had been abandoned on a vast barren plain constricted her body even more than the tightly cinched obi. Incoherent thoughts rushed into her mind all at once: she had not thought of herself as the sort of woman who could weep bitterly like this in front of a man . . . more than anything else, she had disliked being married . . . never once had she taken the initiative to find a husband . . . even after her divorce, she had never felt this kind of sadness . . . she was by nature outspoken about everything, which had played a part in Shūichi's death.

She was unable to restrain her tears. Perhaps being alone with Yūzō had proven even more distressing for Ayako in her present state. Without saying a word, she got up and went to the next room. Untying her obi and taking off her kimono, she stood for a while holding the dress she intended to change into, her gaze fixed vacantly on a corner of the room.

"My wife is going to be hospitalized." Yūzō's voice came from beyond the sliding door. Passing along the veranda, Ayako returned to the room facing the garden.

"It's a uterine tumor."

"Will she be operated on?"

"The doctor says that might not be all. They won't know until they cut her open."

"When will that happen?"

"Next Tuesday. Something's not right about the way she's been losing weight."

Their conversation broke off, and they turned their gaze toward the cherry trees in the garden.

"I remember these cherry blossoms were beautiful at night."

"Yes. The mercury lamp in the garden next door provides just the right illumination."

"That must be really nice."

Yūzō left after reminding Ayako that under no conditions should she take in a boarder. She glanced at the clock—2:00 p.m.—and had just begun putting away dishes in the kitchen when the front doorbell rang. She opened to door to find an unfamiliar young man standing there.

"About this poster, have you already found someone?" Tall and wearing a blue work uniform, he did not look at all like a student.

"No, I just put it up, but I've just about decided against taking someone in after all."

"Decided against it?"

Ayako strode up beside him, tore down the poster, and hurriedly folded it up.

"I was thinking of renting out an upstairs room, but I've suddenly changed my mind."

"Upstairs? You mean the room facing south?" the young man asked, pointing. At Ayako's nod, he broke into a smile and, taking a business card from his breast pocket, bowed politely.

"Will you rent the upstairs room to me just for one night tonight?"

"Just one night?"

"I assure you that I can be trusted. I'll even bring my own bedding. I'll clean up after myself and leave in the morning. I really won't be any bother to you."

It was so sudden that Ayako was at a loss to reply and just studied the young man's features as he bowed repeatedly.

— 27 —

Though he had an easygoing smile and did not appear to be hiding any evil designs, she could not very well agree to rent the upstairs room for just one night. It was not difficult to imagine that this honest-looking young man might undergo some transformation and come after her with a knife in the middle of the night.

"If you only need a room for one night, you could stay at an inn or a hotel, couldn't you? I'm afraid the answer must be no."

"I guess I'm asking too much after all." The young man looked up at the second story with an air of profound disappointment but then said as if it had suddenly occurred to him, "The wire holding that TV antenna is pretty loose. I'll bet your reception is bad. Let me fix it for you. I work at an electrician's shop and can check any other connections in your house and fix them. And I'll pay for your putting me up, so please, won't you rent me the upstairs room just for one night?"

"Why exactly do you want to stay in my house for only one night?" Ayako demanded angrily.

"I'd like to try spending a peaceful night in a neighborhood lined with such stately mansions."

Amused by his way of putting it, Ayako laughed in spite of herself and said, "In that case, would you fix the TV antenna now? The timer on the microwave oven is broken, and the defroster in the refrigerator isn't working properly. If you fix all of those, I might think about it." Just as she was wondering what she had gotten herself into, the young man dashed to the light van parked out front. Returning with his tool bag he strode uninvited into the entranceway. Ayako nervously showed him into the kitchen and pointed at the microwave oven without saying a word.

"I'm not much good at anything else, but when it comes to electricity, I'm something of a genius." True to his word, he repaired it handily after fiddling with it for only five or six minutes. "A dentist lives a little east of here, doesn't he?"

Looking at his wholesome countenance and his close cropped hair, Ayako gradually began to feel calmer. She took a bottle of cola from the refrigerator and poured him a glass. After all he must realize by now that she was home alone, and if he harbored evil designs he would surely have acted on them already.

"That dentist is building a new home next to the hospital, a magnificent three-story house. From the roof I was able to get a good look at your garden."

"What? You could see everything?"

"I couldn't see inside the house, but the cherry trees were in plain sight. They're big, beautiful trees, and . . ." After unplugging the refrigerator and moving it to the middle of the kitchen, he inspected the machinery in back.

"I did all the wiring in that house. For the last five days I've been looking at those cherry trees."

He told her that since the thermostat was "all out of whack" it couldn't be repaired so easily, so before taking that on he would fix the antenna on the roof. Ayako took him upstairs. The eight-mat room facing south that she had in mind for a boarder had been Shūichi's until a year ago. The bookshelves and wardrobe had been left as they were. Three tennis rackets he had cherished from his college years were hanging on the wall. Ayako opened the curtains that had been shut for weeks. A view of the north-south Hankyū and the National Railway lines as well as of the Hanshin line beyond them could be seen from this room. A panorama extending from the base of Mount Rokkō all the way to the sea in distant Kobe opened out with the cherry trees right in the middle.

"Is this the room you'll let to a boarder?" the young man asked Ayako as he stood by the window.

"That was my intention, but I've already decided against it."

As if he had suddenly remembered something, the young man left off looking at the tennis rackets and bookshelves and pulled a five thousand-yen note out of his pocket.

"This is all I've budgeted."

"I still haven't decided whether or not I'll rent it to you."

Responding with a smile, he climbed onto the roof with the wire and cutting pliers.

"Be careful not to fall. This roof's pretty steep."

"Would you mind turning on the TV?" he shouted from overhead. Ayako hurried downstairs and switched on the television. Then she went out into the yard and looked up at the roof.

"How's the reception?"

At that, she went back inside to check. After turning through various channels, she ran back out to the yard and shouted, "It's coming through beautifully."

The young man's face appeared as he looked down from a corner of the roof and then disappeared again. Ayako went upstairs and waited until he came down. Feeling as if she had known him for a very long time, she was in an unusually good mood and decided that if he was so anxious to spend a night in this room that would be fine. When he came down from the roof, his forehead was covered with perspiration. The sunlight glaring off the rooftops of distant houses seemed like that of early summer.

"Was this your son's room?"

Ayako nodded in response to his question and, looking out the window, pointed in the direction of the Ishiya River. "He went out to buy some cigarettes, and right at that corner there he was hit by a car."

"Oh."

"He was killed instantly."

The young man poked his head out the window next to Ayako's and stared at the banks of the Ishiya River. His large, suntanned hands were rough and cracked in places.

"He had just graduated from college and had started working at a commercial firm."

A steady stream of cars was moving along the Hanshin Highway. It was clear, but the sky did not appear blue. Smoke-stacks of factories lined the crooked shore of the harbor out into Osaka Bay. For some time, Ayako and the young man stood side by side gazing at the view from the upstairs window.

"Will you let me stay here tonight?" he asked with a note of hesitation.

"Alright, but just this one night. I won't fix meals for you or do anything else to take care of you."

With a pleased look, the young man left saying he would return that evening with his bedding. After he had gone, Ayako was suddenly beset with a sense of regret for having agreed to his request. Nagged by misgivings, she filled the time until evening with sundry chores, taking in the laundry and clean-ing the kitchen. Several times she found herself standing in front of the telephone holding the business card he had hand-ed her and thinking of calling the electrician's shop and back-ing out of her offer. But each time she hesitated, and in the end she resolved to maintain the agreement. She had promised, after all. He was a cheerful young man, seemed nice enough, and did not appear to have any evil intentions.

A woman in the neighborhood stopped by and invited Ay-ako to go shopping, so the two set out for the market near the station. Her neighbor rattled on and on about her recent volunteer work, about how to make good crepes, about how to make apricot jam, and so on. As Ayako nodded and hemmed in response, Yūzō's face appeared in her mind's eye. She sensed that the purpose of his visit had not solely been the matter of Shūichi's first anniversary services. But after twenty years, Yūzō seemed distant, a total stranger. As she walked along the quiet, petal-strewn hill with her loquacious friend, Ayako could not get one thought out of her mind: Why had she not been able just that once to forgive Yūzō for having become intimate with the young office worker at his company?

Suddenly she had a burning sensation at the nape of her neck. Although it was a nice warm day, the rush of blood from her neck to her cheeks sucked the heat from her waist, her calves, and her feet. After Shūichi's accident, her periods had become irregular and then ended with a very light one three months ago. Ayako was at the age when that was to be expected, but she felt both anxious and irritable with the loss of something elemental within her.

A large bag of bedding was sitting in front of the door to her house. The young man, now wearing a suit, was waiting for her with both hands thrust into his pockets. Ayako said good-bye to her neighbor and approached the front door, rubbing her cold fingers against her flushed cheeks.

The young man greeted Ayako in a booming voice and heaved the heavy bag of bedding onto his shoulder. He quickly deposited it in the upstairs room and came back down.

"You're pretty audacious, aren't you? You'd make a great merchant," Ayako muttered candidly. Behaving in a high-handed manner without giving offense seemed to be a distinctive, inherent quality of this young man.

"I'll be back around eight. Thanks for everything. I'll make sure to fix the refrigerator tomorrow."

Before Ayako had a chance to say anything, the young man hopped into the shop's light van and drove off down the hill.

He showed up a little after eight accompanied by a young woman wearing a plain beige dress. Ayako lost her composure, feeling that she had been handily made a fool of, and sat down in the entranceway to block them. As she was about to say something, the young man spoke first, "This is my wife. We just got married today."

"Today?"

The young woman, who had not the slightest air of wantonness about her but who could not be called attractive, bowed slightly and shyly mumbled a greeting.

"The 'wedding,' such as it was, was just a matter of reporting our marriage to city hall."

With that, he went ahead and led the young woman upstairs by the hand, stealing a sideward glance at Ayako, who was staring at them in disbelief. She felt an inexpressible anger that her own house should be treated as a "love hotel" by complete strangers, and she wanted them to leave. But she lacked the energy to chase upstairs after them and tell them in no uncertain terms to get out. She told herself that the situation was partly redeemed by the fact that there was nothing vulgar about them, and she saw nothing for it but to latch the gate, lock the front door, and return to her room. She had heated the bathwater but didn't feel like getting in. Occasionally she would prick up her ears to determine what was going on upstairs, but the solidly built house prevented any sounds from reaching her. A bluish-white light emanating from the bank president's residence next door covered everything. They had apparently turned on their mercury lamp, and the cherry trees in Ayako's garden loomed out of the darkness.

After ten o'clock, Ayako's ambivalent feelings had subsided enough that she got into the bath. Since retiring she seldom went out, and she rarely put on makeup anymore. The women in the neighborhood kidded her saying that it actually made her look younger. Her face had become puffy and fleshy, but she realized that she was at an age when that added a sort of attractiveness. She suddenly recalled that Yūzō used to like to bathe with her. Whenever she refused, he would immediately fall into a bad mood, and so she would grudgingly follow him into the bathroom where she would remain huddled motionlessly in Yūzō's arms. There was no way she could move about freely in front of a man while naked.

As she was drying herself, she suddenly felt an awful premonition accompanied by the words "lovers' suicide." Worried that the couple upstairs might have some reason to take that irreversible step, Ayako hurriedly got dressed and went to the

— 33 —

bottom of the stairs to try to hear what was going on. But there was no hint of a conversation. In fact, there was no sound at all. She realized that they were not the sort to transform into pilferers or robbers, but it seemed as if something even more alarming was about to happen. The lights in both the upstairs hallway and the room had been turned off, but the pitch darkness no doubt sheltered a young couple, total strangers.

Ayako thought of calling the police. But when she thought of how awkward it would be if her anxieties proved groundless, she hesitated. She returned to her room and absentmindedly laid out a futon on which she sat motionlessly, a light cardigan sweater draped over her nightgown. When the clock passed eleven, she finally resolved to go upstairs. Her heart was beating wildly. Stealthily, she approached the eight-mat room and was about to call out to the couple when she detected their faint voices. They were apparently in bed. Ayako pricked up her ears as she stood in the pitch-dark hallway.

"Now don't fall asleep."

"Mmm." There were signs of motion, and the young man's voice shifted toward the window.

"Come over here."

"No, I'm too embarrassed."

"It's pitch dark. I can't see a thing."

"I'll put something on and then come over."

"It's warm today. You'll be fine naked."

"It's not because I'm cold." The woman's voice also shifted toward the window. Ayako realized that she had been worried about nothing and felt as if strength were draining from her as she relaxed.

"You can see the ocean in the distance and the cherry blossoms in full bloom. We only need to stay one night, and besides it only cost five thousand yen. No matter how much I thought about it, I couldn't see how I was going to be able to fulfill your wishes." The sound of the young woman's muffled laughter echoed in Ayako's heart.

"The cherry blossoms are beautiful, huh?"

"For sure. . . ."

"And you can see the lights of Kobe."

His voice broke off. The woman's laughing was barely audible. The two of them seemed to be hiding their nakedness near the window as they gazed out at the cherry blossoms bathed in the lingering glow of the garden lamps.

"You know what I think? A woman's happiness definitely lies in marrying a rich man."

"Yeah, I think so too."

"You talk as if it had nothing to do with you. Someday, buy me a house like this, okay?"

" . . . Mmm."

"Somehow that response doesn't inspire much confidence."

Ayako quietly descended the stairs. Turning off the light in her room, she opened the glass doors to the veranda. It was a warm night. It occurred to her that it might rain tomorrow. She sat on the veranda for a long time gazing at the blossoms that would perish in the slightest breeze, even without rain. She had never before stared so breathlessly at them. Hemmed with blue light, the enormous cotton-like clusters of pale pink blossoms seemed to float in the air. They appeared as a bewitching living organism that would diminish gradually, trickling away. Since sleep seemed out of the question, Ayako decided to spend this strange night staying up with the cherry trees.

Neither the moon nor any stars were visible, and both the garden stones and the porcelain chairs were hidden in the dark. Only the spectacle of the cherry blossoms against the night sky scattering their petals deeply moved her, and she was intoxicated by the sensation of giving herself over to a warm shower of blossoms. The couple upstairs had no doubt left the window and were back under the quilts. It seemed to Ayako as if she could detect the scent of their bodies. For the longest time she immersed herself in the atmosphere of the blossoms.

Various thoughts crossed her mind, but suddenly one among them stood out. "Oh, is this it?" she thought. She was unable to fathom exactly what "this" was, but she had a feeling that at that very moment she was capable of becoming any sort of woman. Amid that night's blossoms she glimpsed how that might happen, but as soon as she averted her eyes from the cherry trees, the hazy image vanished without a trace.

Eyebrow Pencil

眉墨

My mother in a lavender one-piece dress she had just purchased and my aunt sporting a straw hat with a light blue ribbon were sitting in the back seat of the car, their legs tucked under them, discussing whether or not they had forgotten anything.

Mother said as she waved to her grandchildren, "Oh, never mind. If we're missing anything, we can always buy it there." Early in the morning on the tenth of July, my mother, my aunt, and I set out for Karuizawa. We had planned for a possible stay until the end of September, and so every household item we could think of was crammed into the interior and trunk of the car. My wife and the kids intended to wait until the summer school vacation and join us then.

It was because of my having contracted tuberculosis the previous year that we were spending the summer in Karuizawa. An acquaintance who lived there worried about how the summer heat in Osaka would affect me and urged me to come relax and recuperate, adding that he would rent a house for us. More than my own condition, I was worried about the health of my mother, who during the past few years seemed rather run-down. When I mentioned this to her, she said with a reproachful pout, "It's summer, so of course it's hot! A place like Karuizawa where the rich go—a trip there is more than the likes of us deserve."

But, being a mother, she also worried about my health, and after a while said, "I don't particularly want to go, but if you're determined to, I suppose I'll tag along. You couldn't go three months without someone to fix your meals. As long as we're going, why don't we invite Tome? The summer heat really seems to get to her." She immediately telephoned my aunt, who had lost her son four years earlier and was living by herself in an apartment in Amagasaki. Aunt Tome, the younger sister of my deceased father, accepted the invitation with delight. "As soon as I mentioned Karuizawa, Tome said 'That's where the emperor goes! I never dreamed I'd ever be able to spend three months in such a grand place.'"

When the Karuizawa trip was decided, Mother was suddenly in high spirits and immediately set about stuffing cardboard boxes with things to take along.

In the car, Mother and Aunt Tome talked of nothing but old times. Sitting in the driver's seat listening, I felt it strange that Mother was so free and easy about bringing up things she had never told anyone before. She had once attempted suicide when I was in high school, and now she jabbered on about the circumstances, impatient when the right words wouldn't come to mind.

"He was keeping a woman somewhere, and it had gotten so that he was never around. What's more, the business wasn't going well, and creditors kept coming to our doorstep every day. I just decided to end it all."

"All that must have driven you out of your mind." Plump Aunt Tome chimed in with a note of recollection, her round eyes opening still rounder. Now and then I would glance at the reflection of the two in the rearview mirror.

"This boy was already in high school. He could have made it on his own without me. So, I decided to end it all. Once I made that decision, I thought about where I would die, and decided on your place in Amagasaki. I could make it there by bus in half an hour, and there would be someone there to take care of my remains. So, I bought a bottle of a hundred tablets of Brovarin sleeping pills at a drug store and got on the Hanshin bus. It was hot that day."

"I'm sure your decision to die at my place was fated."

"When I got off at Higashi Naniwa, there was a café right in front of the bus stop. I thought that before I died, I'd have something good to eat, so I went inside and ordered broiled eel over rice and a bottle of saké. It was to be my last drink."

Mother laughed, pressing both hands over her mouth. When she hunched over to laugh, the outline of her frail shoulders showed through the light fabric. In the short space of six months, her weight had gone from ninety-nine pounds down to only seventy-seven. She had been to the hospital for an examination to see if something might be wrong, but she complained only of palpitations and told the doctor that she was otherwise in no pain and did not feel unwell. An electro-cardiogram showed nothing out of the ordinary, so the doctor just gave her something to calm her nerves.

Summer seemed to have arrived in full force that day. As we speeded along the Meishin Expressway I turned on the air conditioner. We got onto the Chūō Highway just before Na-goya, and after a while it became chilly in the car. After pass-ing the Nakatsu River, the mountains of Kiso spread out before us. I turned off the air conditioner and opened the windows.

"After I ate the broiled eel, I thought, 'Well, it's time to die,' and I climbed the stairs to your apartment with that in mind. Luckily, you were out and the door was unlocked. 'OK, now I'll die.' That's what I thought."

"Weren't you afraid?" I asked.

"I wasn't afraid. What frightens me now is to think that I wasn't afraid then." She went on to say that she had given no thought at the time to her only son whom she would leave behind, and that she recalled everything in her life up to that point as if it were all linked like a chain. Her mother died soon after she was born, and she was taken in by the childless couple who ran the bakery next door. That couple sent her out as a domestic servant when she was nine years old. Only later did she realize that her place of employment was what is commonly called a brothel.

"They never called me by my real name; I was known as 'Peewee.' They worked me like a horse from six in the morning until ten or eleven at night. And I was just a nine year-old kid. I feel sorry for myself just thinking about it."

"If you had kept working there, you'd no doubt have grown up to attract a lot of customers."

"I suppose so. I shouldn't have been put in a place like that. Someone advised 'Get her out of there right away,' and I barely managed to get out of a bad situation and return home."

There wasn't much traffic on the Chūō Highway. I had heard that by August it would be jammed with cars headed for Kamikōchi and Karuizawa, but now there were only freight trucks on their regular routes whose drivers operated their rigs with an accustomed air, obeying the speed limit set for the outside lane. Occasionally interrupting herself to bend close to my ear and tell me to slow down, Mother continued her story.

"I was nine, you know. And since they drove me so hard from morning until night, I'd end up dozing off during the day. And then the whores would play mean tricks on me. They'd use a cord to tie my hair to a teakettle and then yell, 'Peewee, you're wanted. Hurry and get up!' I'd jump up in a panic and run half asleep to the madam's room, the teakettle clanging along behind me."

Aunt Tome doubled up with laughter.

"You think it's funny, but even now I can't forget the sound of that teakettle."

I asked, "What kinds of things were you thinking about the moment you swallowed those pills in Aunt Tome's apartment?"

"I wasn't thinking about anything. After lying there for a while, I fell asleep."

"When I got back from the market, I saw your shoes and thought 'Ah, Yuki's here,' and called out to you. But there was no answer. I looked in and thought, 'She's fast asleep.' But something wasn't right. An empty medicine bottle was lying on the floor, and when I shook you and yelled 'Yuki, Yuki,' you opened your eyes slightly and said 'I took the medicine.' Then you fell asleep again."

"You must have been surprised."

"Surprised isn't the word for it! My legs were shaking, my face was twitching, and I don't even remember how I managed to run to a public phone. My fingers were shaking and I couldn't even dial the emergency number."

Ten hours after having been transported to the hospital Mother regained consciousness. After Aunt Tome notified me, I was frightened and spent the night curled up inside a closet in our house. I had a feeling that if I went to the hospital, Mother would die.

Mother said, "Strange things happen, you know. While I was asleep, I had only one dream. I never told anyone about it, but just once I stole some money from the place where I worked as a domestic servant. It had been decades ago and I had never once recalled it, but it came to mind when I was hanging between life and death: the time when I was nine years old and stole some small change from the poorly lit front desk."

Aunt Tome muttered in her usual devil-may-care tone, "We're really the dregs of humanity. We were born into poor families and didn't get decent educations, so we've never amounted to much."

Mother responded in the same tone, "You and me both. I worked and worked, my husband was a pain in the neck, and to top it all off I attempted suicide by taking sleeping pills. Then, before I know it, I'm seventy years old and going to Karuizawa to get away from the heat. It's really a good thing I didn't die then."

We stopped several times along the way to rest, so it was eight o'clock in the evening when we arrived in Karuizawa in thick fog. From the station I called the acquaintance who had arranged for our housing, and he immediately came to meet us. We went back on the highway toward Naka Karuizawa and turned into Shiozawa Street and then down a small lane barely wide enough for one car to pass through at a time. In the woods covered with thick fog, vacation cottages whose owners had not yet arrived were scattered about like dark blots. The cool air suffused with the scent of trees and grasses was bracing, and in the yellow fog of the headlights I somehow sensed that from tomorrow we would have a very good time in Karuizawa.

Located about three hundred feet down the small lane, the house we were renting was a wooden bungalow surrounded by a dense growth of trees. It was laid out with a wooden-floored kitchen and dining area right in the middle flanked by a six-mat tatami room and a bath and toilet. My acquaintance left after handing me the key and mentioning that, since mornings and evenings might get rather chilly, he would bring a kerosene stove the next day. Having stood vacant for a year, the house was damp and musty, but even that put my mind at ease.

Taking a seat in a worn-out rattan chair, Aunt Tome put the straw hat she had been wearing since morning on the table, and complained, "I still have this sensation of rocking. Somehow I don't feel so well."

Mother said, "We spent ten hours riding in a car. You'll feel better after a good night's rest. I feel great. You wouldn't think so by looking at me, but I'm tough when it comes to riding in a car." She began unpacking her luggage, for a while busy emptying the cardboard boxes of their contents. She suddenly gasped and turned to me.

"I've forgotten my eyebrow pencil."

"Your eyebrow pencil?"

"What should I do? I have to have it!"

"You can get by without it for one night, can't you?"

Mother pressed her hands together in a pleading gesture, "Wouldn't there be a cosmetics shop somewhere near the station? I'll go buy some now, so please drive me there."

Mother countered my reluctance with repeated pleas. Leaving Aunt Tome, who had already gone to bed, I drove with Mother again to the front of Karuizawa Station. The fog was even thicker, and only the taillights of the cars in front of us were dimly gleaming. Right in front of the station was a variety store where a small illuminated sign proclaimed: "Name-brand cosmetics."

It had been a year or two since Mother had gotten into the habit of painting her eyebrows before going to bed. Her hair was now completely white, and even her eyebrows had become hoary. She dyed her hair black, but she couldn't very well do the same to her eyebrows. She left them white during the day, but before getting into bed she would sit on the quilt with her legs tucked under her and carefully paint her brows. When my wife and I asked her why she did that, she would just laugh with embarrassment and not answer.

While waiting for Mother to come out of the variety store, I got out of the car and took a good first look at Karuizawa. On both sides of the avenue extending from the front of the station I could see what looked like cafés and stores selling Western items, but all was enveloped in fog, and I couldn't make out any human figures. The sweater I had on was damp and smelled faintly of yarn. Suddenly everything seemed somber, but I assured myself that my spirits would brighten in the morning when the fog lifted and I would see bright sunlight filtering through the trees. A train, apparently from Ueno, stopped at the station, but only a few people got off.

The weather was pleasant the following day, and we ate breakfast on the veranda, looking at the sunlight pouring down in striped patterns. Aunt Tome was in good spirits again, and had arranged in a milk bottle some flowers she had picked strolling about here and there by herself early that morning. This time it was Mother who complained of stomach problems. She spent most of the morning pressing her hand against her left side, her face screwed up in pain.

"Your stomach is just reacting to being rocked so long in the car. You'll feel better soon." With that assurance from Aunt Tome, Mother slowly got up from the rattan chair, and the two of them went out to pick flowers. I spent the whole afternoon reading. After tiring of that, I went to a café halfway down Shiozawa Street and had a cup of coffee. Three days passed in that fashion. The weather was good during that time, and I was delighted at the thought that I would surely recover that summer.

The morning of the fifth day after our arrival in Karuizawa began with heavy rainfall, of a sudden making the scenery around the house gloomy. All around were leafy treetops darkened by the dampness, and we were enveloped in shadows and stillness as if our little house were off by itself somewhere in the depths of a mountain. We had to have the kerosene heater on all day, and both mother and Aunt Tome, their knees covered with blankets, did nothing but gaze through the window at the pouring rain.

Mother mumbled, "I wonder if there isn't a hospital somewhere close by."

"Does your stomach still hurt?"

Mother, a forlorn look on her face, answered with a nod. She said that it was not unbearable, but that it was a nasty pain, one she had never experienced before. "Here I've come all the way to Karuizawa, and this is no fun at all."

I telephoned my acquaintance and told him about the situation. I asked if there was a hospital in the vicinity and learned that there was a large one, Karuizawa Hospital, only five minutes by car from where we were. I drove Mother there. There was little sign of life on the streets, but the hospital was packed. After the examination, Mother came out and said with a note of dejection, "Tomorrow I'll need to take barium and have x-rays taken of my stomach."

The next day when I awoke, Aunt Tome was sitting alone in the rattan chair on the veranda reading a newspaper. Mother was nowhere to be seen. Aunt Tome told me that since it wasn't much of a distance to walk, Mother had gone to the hospital by herself. The rain had stopped, but a mist hung over everything. The cry of a cuckoo could be heard nearby, and Aunt Tome was excited to have noticed a squirrel leaping from branch to branch. Mother returned just as I was wondering whether or not I ought to go pick her up. As soon as she saw me, she said, "It seems I have cancer."

I stared at her for a while without speaking. There was no trace of despondency in her countenance, and it almost seemed as if she must be joking.

"Is that what the doctor said?"

"He didn't say so, but it was written all over his face. That doctor is a lousy liar. He had a big smile, and when I asked him if it was cancer, his eyes popped open wide and he dodged the question, and said, 'So then, have your son come by later. . . .'"

I hurried to the hospital. I identified myself to a nurse and was immediately called into the examination room. The young doctor had a nurse bring the x-ray films to show me.

"It's this right here." The doctor pointed to a dark shadow about an inch in diameter appearing clearly in the middle of the stomach. "When I examined her yesterday with my hand, I could feel it. So I had these taken. Judging from my impression of the shadow and from the way it swells, it doesn't seem likely to be an ulcer."

"My mother said to me 'It seems I have cancer. . . .'" I cast a somewhat accusatory glance at the doctor. Just as Mother described, his eyes popped open wide and he mumbled. He seemed like a decent man, but his eyes somehow lacked sincerity.

"I'm sure I didn't say anything like that," he said defending himself. Then he turned his eyes to the film and muttered, "But, it's true. Tomorrow, we'll examine her with a gastrocamera and take a tissue sample, but I don't think there's any mistake."

"Then, you'll operate, won't you?"

"Of course it must be taken out."

"After surgery, will she get better?"

"I think it's in a fairly early stage, but until we cut it out, we can't be sure."

For a long time I stared vacantly at the doctor's shoulder. I wanted to return immediately to Osaka. The doctor looked at Mother's chart, and asked, "I understand that you're here from Osaka. What would you like to do? Will you have the surgery here, or go back to Osaka?"

"Which do you think is better?"

"It depends on your circumstances, but considering care for her after the surgery, I would recommend doing it here where the climate is better."

"With cancer, I've heard that when it starts to hurt, it's already too late."

"I don't think her stomach pains were caused by this cancer. It hasn't yet progressed to that point. It probably began to hurt for some other reason, and that's why she decided to come to the hospital."

"My mother is seventy years old. Will she be able to stand surgery at that age?"

"At seventy, she's still young," the doctor laughed. "It won't be any problem. That is, as long as she doesn't have other physical problems. We'll examine her for those things too."

When I left the hospital, the mists had cleared and the sun was shining softly. Perhaps it was my imagination, but there seemed to be more cars on the highway. Some young women passed by on bicycles. The cosmos that had just begun bloom-ing by the side of the road were bending in the cool wind. Ka-ruizawa's summer had begun. I turned down Shiozawa Street, which was lined endlessly on both sides by the dense green of trees, and pulling over by the side of the road, smoked a ciga-rette. There could hardly be any doubt that it was cancer. For a long time I sat in the driver's seat pondering whether to return to Osaka or to remain in Karuizawa for the surgery.

Some children holding a butterfly net were staring at the roof of my car. I poked my head out the window and saw a large black butterfly resting there. The children's eyes were fixed on that butterfly, but they were holding back because of me. Several young women in tennis wear came by on bicycles and called out, "Oh, what a huge butterfly!" "Go for it, kiddo!"

Apparently startled by the young women, the butterfly flit-ted above the heads of the children and disappeared into the forest. Keeping a close watch on it and stooping low, the chil-dren ran after it.

No matter how certain Mother might be that she had can-cer, I determined that I would continue to feign ignorance. Gazing at the depth of the forest into which both butterfly and children had disappeared, I repeated this resolution to myself again and again. My father, who had died ten years previously, suddenly came to mind. He often beat my mother. When I was a child, I felt nothing but fear for a father like that, but as I grew older I came to despise him. "All those times you hit my defenseless mother as hard as you could, didn't you?" I came to view him with such an accusation in my eyes. And until he died, I continued to despise him. But as I stared blankly at the flickering sunlight in the abundant greenery, for some reason I wanted to cling to him and reproached myself for despising him. I have no idea why I was overcome by such a feeling.

Setting out again, I turned down the small lane, proceeding slowly toward our house. I saw an elderly woman standing in the road in front of me, a cane in one hand and a small package in the other. She was of slight stature and wore a brown kimono and a knitted *haori* of the same color. She seemed to be peering into our house, and when I got out of the car, she bowed her head hesitantly.

"What can I do for you?" I asked as I approached her. She pointed to the tasteful villa with the triangular roof behind our house, identifying herself as Mrs. Murakoshi and saying that as a gesture to make our acquaintance she had brought a few walnuts.

"I've caught a few glimpses of elderly people, and thought that as fellow old folk, we might be able to enjoy one another's company."

I thanked her and accepted the package of walnuts. "My mother and my aunt are here, but since our arrival my mother has not felt well and has been down in bed all this time."

"Oh, that's too bad! How old is she?"

"Seventy."

"I'm eighty-four. It's been nearly twenty years since I started coming to Karuizawa, but rainy seasons this long have been rare."

Mrs. Murakoshi's disappointment was registered in a glance at me, then with a tottering gait she started back home down a small path. I somehow felt apologetic and started walking abreast with her. We soon entered an even narrower path extending to the left and leading through a grove interspersed with white birch. It was covered with newly fallen green leaves over a thick layer of leaf mold.

"I came here in April, so I've been lonely now for several months. Others who come here every year are mostly young and not interested in associating with old folk like me."

"Do you live alone?" I asked.

"I have a maid, but we don't talk much."

"If my mother felt better, you and she could be good company for each other."

Apparently noticing my accent, Mrs. Murakoshi stopped and looked at me with a smile.

"So, are you here from western Japan?"

"Yes, Osaka."

"It's too bad, isn't it, that she's unwell after coming from so far." She said that she came to Karuizawa every year in April and stayed until around the beginning of November. The place isn't the way it used to be; now it's crowded in the summer and too noisy. She explained that she stayed from April to November because she liked Karuizawa in the early summer and in the autumn.

"Doesn't your family come to visit?"

She cocked her head slightly and answered, "They come once in a while, but they don't stay at the villa. They just get a room at the Mampei Hotel."

There were obviously some family circumstances, and it would have been indelicate to pursue the matter further. Then Mrs. Murakoshi pointed beyond the forest.

"From here you can see the sun set. It's nice to see the morning sun filtering through the trees, but the way the rays of the setting sun bleed through the leaves is really splendid."

When I got home I told Mother that an elderly lady named Murakoshi had come to visit and brought some walnuts.

"What's she like?"

"She seems very refined. She said she's been coming to Karuizawa for twenty years now."

"Is her manner of speech affected?"

"No, not at all. But she does use polite language."

"Hmm, that's good. I wouldn't know how to respond to affected speech since I've never associated with people like that." Then Mother asked what the doctor had said.

"It's nothing like cancer. It's an ulcer. But medicine alone won't cure it. They'll probably have to operate. That's what he said."

"An operation . . ."

"What do you want to do? Do you want to go back to Osaka, or have the operation here?"

Mother was lost in thought for a while then suddenly looked up and stared straight into my eyes. "You're good at lying to outsiders, but you never could lie to me." I went out into the garden and ate the walnuts Mrs. Murakoshi had given us, cracking them with a rock.

The next morning, Mother and I headed once again in the car for Karuizawa Hospital. Aunt Tome, who said that she couldn't remain calm waiting by herself, got in with us. As we turned off Shiozawa Street onto the national highway, a policeman standing there ordered us to stop.

"A member of the imperial family is about to pass down this highway. I'm sorry, but you'll have to wait a while."

The policeman was receiving communications through a transceiver in his ear. We were stopped for rather a long time. The policeman again came running up.

"They've just passed through Naka Karuizawa. It won't be long, so please wait."

It appeared that we would be very late for our appointment with the doctor. I was angry but just remained silent and smoked one cigarette after another. On the highway were scores of cars that had been ordered to stop. Disgust could be read on every face that would occasionally protrude out of windows as drivers waited for the imperial family member to pass. Aunt Tome said, "What a gap between them and us. We're born as the same human beings."

"No kidding. As soon as I was born I was given away. At nine I went to work at a brothel and had a teakettle tied to my hair. 'What a gap' isn't the word for it."

Mother laughed, finding it all very amusing. Then, from behind she pressed both hands against my cheeks as I was sullenly gripping the steering wheel and softly whispered, "Don't worry. It's okay if I live, and it's also okay if I die. That's really how I feel."

The car of the imperial household had apparently passed, and traffic on the national highway slowly began to move. The policeman came running up and bowed. "They have passed. Please proceed."

After the examination with the gastrocamera, Mother returned exhausted to the waiting room.

"I'm not a stone. They have their nerve making a human being swallow something like that."

We were kept waiting for an hour, and then I was called in. It was not the young doctor of yesterday, but the middle-aged head surgeon who offered an explanation.

"In the examination room, I told your mother that it was an advanced ulcer."

"But it's something else, right?"

"Yes, it's something else. I think it's exactly what the internist told you yesterday. It will take five or six days for the results from the tissue sample. If you're going to have the surgery done here, I'd like to have her admitted right away, today even."

"We'll probably have the surgery performed here, but could you wait two or three days before she's admitted?"

I wanted to have my family come immediately. The children were not yet out for summer vacation, but I thought we ought to have them excused from classes. When we got home, I called my wife. "It's turned out that she'll have surgery after all." Mother was at my side, her gaze fixed on me.

"Tomorrow we'll take the bullet train to Tokyo, and get a train from Ueno," my wife said. Then she asked, "It's an ulcer, isn't it?" I didn't answer, and she understood by my silence. She let out what amounted to a shriek and began crying at the other end of the line.

Mother spent all that day in bed. Several times I said to her, "Mom, it's a good thing it's just an ulcer. You're lucky." Each time she would smile and nod. That evening when she got up, we began to hear and feel a distant rumble. I went to the small path where I had walked with Mrs. Murakoshi the day before.

Rays of the setting sun filtered through the branches of trees, filling the narrow path with a surfeit of light. For a long time I stood in that crimson glow looking fixedly at the sun sinking beyond the forest. It seemed as if an elderly woman with a cane would come out to see the setting sun, but no one came. The stillness was broken intermittently only by a sound like the firing of a cannon.

Even after night fell, the sound continued. Aunt Tome came out and called to me.

"They're putting on some really beautiful fireworks."

I unfolded a brochure I had picked up in a coffee shop showing summer events in Karuizawa. A fireworks display was scheduled for the sixteenth of July.

"It's over in the direction of Sengataki."

Blocked by the forest, only small fragments of the fireworks were visible from where we were. Mother asked me to take her someplace where we could get a good view of them. "It's been years since I saw fireworks."

We sped in the car toward the launching site, and as we proceeded on the national highway toward Sengataki, Mother cried out, "That's a good spot over there. You can stop the car there."

Following her directions, I turned to the right and entered an area with lawns and flower beds. After stopping, we realized that it was the front yard of Karuizawa Hospital.

"We seem to have a karmic bond with this hospital," Mother muttered and sat down on a handkerchief she had spread on the lawn. Aunt Tome and I followed suit and sat down beside her. The patients had also brought chairs out onto the hospital veranda to watch the fireworks, which were on a grander scale than I had expected, going on endlessly.

"That one's a chrysanthemum. Oh, and that one's a weeping willow." Mother seemed quite gleeful. The night breeze over the plateau disheveled her dyed hair. Motionless as a statue, she sat leaning to the side, her gaunt neck lifted up and her gaze fixed on the sky. The fireworks would come to a lull and then would suddenly start up again. The heavy sound of an explosion would follow a whizzing, then countless colors would burst forth. We were wondering how much longer it would last. The blackness of the sky silently spread out, and we said "Well, let's go home" and started to get up. Just then great bursts of color again appeared without end. I stared at Mother's slight frame from behind. Her remark "It's okay if I live, and it's also okay if I die" grew in my heart and filled me. I turned those words over and over in my mind. There was no doubt she really meant it. Tears welled up in my eyes, blurring the fireworks. I stealthily wiped my eyes with my finger so that Aunt Tome wouldn't notice, but a steady stream kept running down my face. But I did not feel sad.

It was past ten when we returned home. On the way we stopped at a fruit shop and bought five peaches because Mother said that she wanted to reciprocate Mrs. Murakoshi's kindness. Aunt Tome suggested that I wait until tomorrow to deliver them, but relying on the beam of a flashlight I set out down the small path with the peaches in a paper bag. Mrs. Murakoshi's villa was on a larger lot than I had imagined, and I wasn't certain where the entrance was. Making my way along the edge of the forest, I unexpectedly came to some stone gate pillars. Mrs. Murakoshi, who had brought a chair out to her front porch and had been looking up at the night sky, now stared with suspicion at the beam of the approaching flashlight. I stopped, directed the beam at my own face, and apologized for calling on her so late.

"Oh, that's very kind of you. I'm afraid I've made you feel obligated." She seemed glad to have a visitor and pressed me to come inside, but I begged off saying that I couldn't stay. I mentioned that we had just been to see the fireworks.

"Really? I've been sitting here watching them myself. The trees block the view here, but even so now and then I can enjoy one that goes high in the sky." Then she added with a note of regret that, although the fireworks display is held yearly, she always just watched from the front porch of her villa and had never actually gone to see the whole show. It occurred to me that we ought to have invited her to go with us.

"If it turns out that we come here again next year, we'll be sure to invite you to go along."

She looked at me and laughed softly. "I hope we can meet again next year." She smelled the fragrance of the peaches. "There seem to be fewer stars this summer." She heaved a long sigh, and set the peaches on her lap.

I took my leave and, one hand in a trouser pocket, started home along the path soft with a thick layer of fallen leaves. From deep within the forest I could hear the sound of my own footsteps treading the rotting leaves, like some kind of voice whispering to me from ahead. Though it couldn't have been more than a five-minute walk even at a slow pace, I was in such a state of mind that it was an unbearably long and frightening path through the night.

I took a bath, sat down on the rattan chair on the veranda, and was looking out toward the grove of trees illuminated blue by the light trap when I suddenly became aware that Aunt Tome was standing behind me. She asked timidly, "Isn't what's wrong with your mother really cancer?"

"No, it isn't."

The tension went out of her shoulders as if she were relieved. She said good night and went to her own room. For a while I sat there on the veranda, filling my lungs with the chilled, bracing air. On the other side of the small path, a light was on in the villa belonging to some Germans. There were villas here and there that I had supposed until yesterday were vacant, but as I peered into the darkness and saw the faint glow of their light traps, I realized that their owners had come.

I felt worried about Mother and quietly looked into her room. She had changed into a nightgown and, sitting on the quilts with her legs tucked under her, was applying eyebrow pencil. Facing the light, her image was reflected in a small mirror attached to the case, and with pursed lips she was absorbed in painting her brows.

Strength

力

A BOY PUMPING THE pedals of his bicycle disappeared on the other side of the fountain, stirring up dead leaves as he went. Clouds blocked the setting sun, darkening the park and prompting those sitting on benches to get up. It occurred to me, too, that it was about time to leave. Dusk was like a symbol of disappointment that had begun eating away at the park, and the usually refreshing autumn wind instead produced a chill. As I was about to get up, the old man sitting next to me said, "Your work is tough, huh?"

Though it was still autumn, he was wearing knitted gloves. He had a walking stick and wore canvas shoes. Over his stooped back was a dark gray jumper that looked like a real period piece, and its fraying wristbands made me think, *Ah yes, toward evening down-and-out old men like this always show up in parks.* I had deliberately been sitting with my back to him in order to avoid meeting his eyes. But having been suddenly addressed, I couldn't very well leave without acknowledging him, and replied looking over my shoulder, "Yeah, I suppose." It was an annoyance, though, to be drawn into conversation, and I looked down at his walking stick rather than at him. The handle of the stick was covered with gold ornamentation and inlaid with ivory, manifesting superior quality. Once again I ran my eyes over his attire. Though showing evidence of ample use and wear and tear, the jumper, gloves, and trousers were not cheap items.

"Even before it sets, whenever the sun hides behind clouds everyone leaves the park for some reason. It's the same in spring and summer. Strange, huh?" No sooner had he said that than the sinking sun again appeared, bathing the fallen leaves, the bench, and his canvas shoes in a rosy hue. I was no doubt dyed the same color.

"Whenever you're depressed, the best thing for it is to recall your childhood. That's the secret to cheering yourself up."

"Do I look depressed?"

The old man just answered with a smile. Without another word, he slowly stood up and nodded slightly toward me, then with one solid step at a time disappeared down the path strewn with dead leaves. It was true: I had been depressed that entire day. Otherwise I would not have been spending the twilight hours of a workday sitting on a park bench. There were plenty of things getting me down: lack of sleep, the breakdown of business negotiations that were just being finalized, my wife's miscarriage, having to come up with money to make reparations for the many scratches my three-year-old daughter had made on a new car our next-door neighbors had just purchased. . . . But it just so happened that all of these things occurred together; taken singly, none of them amounted to more than one of the petty misfortunes that are common in life, and none was insoluble.

Even so, I was horribly depressed. Like someone who had become fully aware of his failure in life—or, like someone who, contrary to his own will and manipulated by some demonic force, has committed a crime—I had fallen into a deep dejection. After leaving the office, I had not made my planned visit to a client but had just killed time in a coffee shop and trudged about alleys. Before I knew it I had ended up in this park.

In the park now nearly devoid of people, thinking there might be another twenty minutes of sunlight I again sat down on the bench and smoked a cigarette. I harbored a feeling of loathing for the old man who had disappeared down the row of poplars beyond the fountain. He must make it a daily routine to walk about in parks keeping a malicious lookout for people in low spirits. And when he found some prey he would approach and stealthily whisper to them a way to lose even more vitality: recall your own childhood. A time when you were innocent, a time when you imagined nothing for your future but happiness, a time when unpleasant things—rain or thunder, unbearable hot or cold—were suitable pretexts for seeking refuge in the bosom of someone who would protect you.

What could come of recalling such a time in your life? You could never return to it, so wouldn't recalling it just add to the burden of your nostalgia and disappointment? But even as I dismissed such musings, before long things from my juvenile years began to emerge faintly in my mind, not turning into vivid images, but wavering uncannily like particles floating beyond a mist. Memories of childhood . . . There are so many of them, and I can't remember what my face looked like then, so it was impossible even to recall which daydream I was indulging in.

I lit another cigarette without any desire to smoke it, and glanced at the spray of the fountain. Dragged along by a dog on a chain, a boy dug in his heels in an effort to stop, causing the animal to gouge the gravel without moving forward. With labored heaving, the dog tried all the same to move ahead. The boy bent over and finally yielded, again dragged off by the dog. In an instant, in front of the fountain in the vacated park I could see myself from behind: a first grader in elementary school walking nimbly along with a satchel on my back. Rather than "appearing," the image may have been something I made bold to place there. I fixed my gaze on my seven-year-old self, which stood alone in a ruddy-hued universe.

On the day of the entrance ceremony, I of course passed through the school gate in my mother's tow. But the next day, too, she accompanied me to school and came to pick me up afterwards. Our family lived on the westernmost fringe of Osaka's Kita Ward. The kids in the neighborhood all walked to an elementary school fifteen minutes away, but it was my father's wish that I be enrolled in Sonezaki Elementary School, which entailed commuting by bus. Located right in the middle of an amusement district, the school had the highest standards of any in Kita Ward and was a gateway to elite high schools for the college-bound. But from my earliest years I was always getting lost, sending my parents into a panic, so their greatest worry was whether or not I would ever be able to commute safely by myself on the bus.

"There won't be any problem while he's on the bus. Anyway, if he just gets off at the last stop. . . ." One night a few days before the entrance ceremony, my drowsy ears picked up the voice of my drunken father on the other side of the fusuma sliding door.

"That kid wanders aimlessly, so the problem starts when he gets off the bus. Take him there and pick him up for about a week. Even he will get the hang of it."

"Yeah, if I go with him for a week, he should be able to go by himself after that without getting lost. But since it's in the new Sonezaki district, there are lots of alleys. Could he make it to the school without veering off somewhere? He's likely to do that sort of thing."

"Why does that kid end up going in an opposite direction? It's some kind of sickness, I tell you. What's he thinking?"

"It's because you spoiled him. That's why he turned out to be such a pampered son of a poor man."

The words "poor man" apparently rubbed Dad the wrong way.

"You think you understand how things are gonna turn out in life? Maybe I'm stagnating right now in a place like this, but I've never let my wife and child go hungry. Whaddya mean by 'poor man'? Huh? Just what's a 'poor man'?"

Dad's voice was rough, and I started to worry that he might hit Mom again. She also seemed to think that she had really stepped in it and tried to save the situation by muttering, "Well, he couldn't very well be called the pampered son of a rich man."

"Oh, so then, whaddya mean by 'rich man'? By 'rich man,' you mean someone who dresses smart and lives in a big house. You're probably jealous of Kaizuka's wife."

"Let's not talk about that. How many times must you insist on bringing that up?"

Kaizuka was an associate whose double-crossing had been a direct cause of the failure of Dad's business. I knew that my parents' nightly quarrels always started with the name "Kaizuka," so I slipped out from under the quilts, opened the fusuma, and pleaded, "Dad, don't hit Mom." But Dad just glanced at me and continued in an even rougher tone of voice.

"Are you jealous of Kaizuka's wife? Just take a look at her fox-like face. A woman like that paints herself with rouge and powder but has a filthy cunt."

"Don't use that kind of language in front of a child!" Frowning, Mom stood up and whispered that she was going to put me to bed. "Hurry up and go to sleep. If you don't get in the habit of going to bed and getting up early, you'll be in a fix when you start school."

"Don't fight with Dad, OK?"

Nodding in agreement, Mom closed the fusuma and returned to the next room.

"The bus stops across from Osaka Station, right in front of the Hanshin Department Store. If he crosses with the traffic light at Midōsuji and goes straight down the street to the side of the Sonezaki Police Station, he'll come out right in front of the school gate. Even that kid'll get it if you go with him for three days."

Attempting to avert an unfavorable turn in the course of the conversation, Mom steered it back to where it had been.

"You say 'if he goes straight,' but the problem is that kid never goes straight."

"An odd kid!" Dad laughed. I felt relieved, and fell asleep.

Mom went with me only on the day of the entrance ceremony and the day after that. She would tap me on the head to fix my wandering eyes and spoon-feed me instructions: "This is the Hanshin Department Store. Wait until the light turns green and then cross this street." I did exactly as she said.

"Now, we've crossed the street. This brown building is the police station."

Mom led me by the hand about ten meters south on the sidewalk and stopped, pointing at a narrow alley.

"It's the first alley. You turn here. Turn left. That's left, not right. If you turn right, you'll be run over."

"I know that."

"Even if you know it, you're the kind of kid who would turn the wrong way."

We went down the alley. It was about time for school to start, and older pupils and those whose brand-new caps and satchels like mine showed it was their first day were rushing past us. Mom said in a firm tone of voice, "Anyway, you go straight down this street." On the right was an alley that led to bars, small eateries, and pachinko parlors. Mom commanded that I was absolutely not to go down such lanes and intimidated me saying that if I did there were lots of scary men who would take me far away, never to return.

After class the following day, I found Mom standing by the school gate with a worried look on her face. She had gone home after taking me to school and then had gotten back on the bus to come pick me up. In the same tone as that morning, she instructed me about the return trip. When we reached the Hanshin Department Store, she said, "This is where you got off. You mustn't wait for the bus here. Look, a little further over there, you see that bus stop with the number 52? Get on the bus there, show the conductor your commuter pass, and say, 'I get off at this place, so please let me know when we arrive.' You can say that, can't you? Try saying it."

I took out the pass holder that was securely tied to my satchel and repeated the words just as Mom had said them.

The next day, the time finally came for me to go to school by myself. Both yesterday and the day before a woman had been standing at the stop waiting for the bus, which arrived after crossing a bridge. It was crowded when I got on, and I threaded my way through adult legs to get near the driver's seat. I wasn't the least afraid and took the pass holder out of my satchel. It occurred to me that as long as I had that pass I could ride the bus as many times as I wanted in a day even if I had no money. I stared at its numbers and unfamiliar characters, glanced at the driver's handling of the steering wheel, and gazed at the scenes outside the bus. By braiding three thick strands of fishing line together Dad had made a long cord to fasten my pass holder to the metal fittings on my satchel. Grasping the cord, I was swinging the holder about with all my might when it struck the hand of an elderly man in one of the seats.

"Hey!" The old man chided sharply, pressing the back of his assaulted hand. "Don't you know it's dangerous to swing that thing around?" His rebuke caught me off guard, and I turned my back to him. The bus turned left from Umeda New Street and headed down Midōsuji toward Osaka Station.

"That sure is a big cap!" Smiling, the same old man touched my cap. "Couldn't you find a smaller one?"

Even after stuffing the smallest cap available with newspaper, it still fell down below my eyebrows.

"This was the smallest."

Several of the adults around us laughed. I hung my head in embarrassment, causing the cap to slide down and cover my eyes. The adults laughed again. A young man who looked like an office worker took the cap off my head and, folding his newspaper into a sort of wreath, pushed it into the sweatband. Since my father had already done that, the additional newspaper stuck rather far out of the sweatband, but at least the cap stayed on my forehead without falling down. I said in a loud voice, "Thanks!"

"What a little face! Now it looks like a cap on a mushroom." This time, even more people than before looked and me and laughed. I hated being told that I was skinny, and that I had a small face.

"There are three kids in the third class of first-graders that are smaller than me!" I must have sounded pretty earnest because even the driver looked around and laughed.

The sidewalk was bathed in the spring morning sunlight, and after getting off the bus, I stood there and put the pass holder away in my satchel. I could have accomplished that by reaching behind with one hand, but I took the trouble of taking the satchel off my shoulders, setting it on the ground, and putting the holder all the way in the bottom. I was clumsy and needed a lot of time to perform tasks that would present no difficulty for other kids, whether it was buttoning up clothing, finishing a meal, or putting on socks. I tried to put the satchel back over my shoulders, but it didn't go well; the cuff of my jacket caught on the metal parts, pulling the sleeve clear up to my elbow, and I wasn't able to straighten it no matter how much I pulled. I took the satchel off again and set it down. Then I sat down on the sidewalk myself, so that the satchel and I were of the same height. Nearly ten minutes passed before I was finally able to get it situated properly on my back.

I set off toward Midōsuji, intimidated by the buildings, the cars, and the crowds of people. Yesterday and the day before when Mom was with me all of those things were merely novel and pleasant sights, but now that I was by myself they had metamorphosed and seemed like coldly indifferent apparitions. For a moment I came to a stop. A man wearing a headband and workman's split-toed shoes brushed against me as he hurried past. He tripped on something and tottered, dropping the aluminum lunchbox he had under his arm. Clumps of rice, several dried sardines, and a pickled plum scattered on the sidewalk. It seemed that the single rubber band holding the lid of the lunchbox in place had broken in the fall, spilling the contents. The man crawled about on the ground, picking up the dirty rice and gathering the dried sardines and pickled plum. He stuffed them back into the lunchbox and ran across the street before the light changed. The moment he reached the other side, the light turned red. I looked at the grains of rice that had been left behind. The piteous look on the man's face when he abandoned the task made me feel all the lonelier.

On the right, I could see the show windows of the Hanshin Department Store, where several men were dressing a mannequin. I ran up to the window and watched them work. The light had turned green, so I crossed Midōsuji and turned right in front of the Sonezaki Police Station. A grimy old man with a large wicker basket on his back was gathering cigarette butts. With the nib of a pen tied to a long stick, the old man walked on the right, sometimes veering to the left to spear butts. When I tried to get out of his way by going to the right, he also went to the right. When I went to the left, he likewise went to the left. Determined somehow or other to get past the old man, the moment he went next to the wall of the police station, I ran around him as fast as I could go. No matter how far I went, the alley Mom had directed me to was nowhere to be found. When I raced past the butt-gathering old man, I ended up passing the alley I was supposed to turn down. Looking back, I decided to wait until he worked his way past me. He got closer and closer. I leaned against the trunk of one of the ginkgo trees lining the street, trying to stay out of sight of the old man. He saw me when he speared a butt lying at my feet. He stared at me without blinking and, pointing at me, suddenly shouted, "Hey, you! Why haven't you written me even one letter?"

I slipped behind the ginkgo tree and escaped to the front of the police station. If a group of what appeared to be pupils at my school hadn't crossed with the traffic light right at that moment, I probably would have lost all sense of direction, and who knows where I might have ended up? I followed behind those pupils who, I guessed, were in a higher grade. When we turned down the alley off the police station, I saw the familiar black curtains of a pawnshop. The alley was dark and seemed like one from which I'd never return once I entered. But the older pupils continued walking, so I followed since I had nowhere else to go. Under an eave lay a man stripped to the waist.

"Ooh! He's dead, he's dead!" One of the older pupils taunted gleefully.

"Whaaat! Which one of you just said that I'm dead?" His breath reeking of liquor, the man straightened himself up and shouted. With an experienced air, the older pupils slipped past the man. I ran too, determined not to be left behind.

"Every day, you're there dead, aren't you?" the same pupil said as he made a face. The man tried to chase us on unsteady legs but fell back on his buttocks and remained there lying in the street.

One of the others said, "Die! Die! Why don't you just die?" The man just squirmed as he lay there. One of the older pupils gave me an order, "You say it too."

"Die! Die! Why don't you just die?" Before I finished saying those words, the older pupils let out a hurrah and ran scrambling down the alley toward the school gate. I ran after them in a panic. I passed through the school gate and, out of breath, entered my classroom at the end of the first floor.

Now, when my aged mother reminisces about my father, whose life ended in poverty, she does so with a mixture of affection and venom. The malice owes mainly to the ruinousness of his drinking habit and to the fact that during our financial hardships he had secretly kept a mistress. One source of her tender feelings for him was the way he lavished affection on his only son and the scale of that lavishing. Before recalling what happened that day, she noted that it wasn't that she had kept her memories from me but that she had simply forgotten about it.

"That day, your father told me, 'Follow after him and keep an eye on him.' When the bus came, I dashed from our house to the stop and got on in the very back. You were swinging your pass holder around, and when you got off, you sat down on the ground and readjusted the satchel on your back. Then, even though you could have been late for school, you kept looking for the longest time at a man who had dropped his lunchbox, and I wondered whether I ought not just to come out of the crowd and take you to school. But since your father had told me not to let you know I was following you unless absolutely necessary, I kept hidden in the background, wringing my hands.

"Then, once you finally started walking, you traipsed over to look at the show window of a department store. And just when I was relieved that you had made it safely across the intersection with the traffic light, you dashed past an old man gathering cigarette butts, running in the opposite direction. When the old man made some senseless remark to you, you shot back like a bullet in the other direction. I couldn't stand it any longer and called out to you. But you didn't hear me. When you shouted at some guy who was completely soused 'Die! Die! Why don't you just die?' my knees started shaking."

At the conclusion of her speech, Mom added, smiling and with tears in her eyes, "After I saw you safely into the school gates, I went back home and described the whole thing to your father from start to finish. He laughed so hard he was holding his sides. After his business failed, that was the only time I saw him laugh like that. 'That's great, that's just great. There's hope that even that nitwit will make it in life.' Then he waited on tenterhooks until you came back home."

I looked at the fountain. The image of myself had disappeared. Sometime it may appear again and start walking about. But it was based on what I had heard from my mother only a year before and was the imaginative product of a mind in which sentimentalism and intoxication were mixed together one evening. The juvenile image of myself went back down the alley that *is* myself.

The Lift

五千回の生死

TONIGHT I'M DRUNK FOR the first time in a long time. Of course, when night comes around I usually imbibe, but it's been a long time since I got this comfortably drunk. So let me share a story I've been saving. After all, it's been several years since I've been pleasantly drunk and have had a conversation partner like you. It's just been work, work, work. Sundays and holidays too, you know. It was five years ago that I finally managed to get my own small office, a room in an enormous building with rental space. It's the sort of design office that could go under anytime, where I have to do everything myself—from rough sketches to pasteup. I could count on one hand the days I've been able to get home before ten o'clock. By the time I come home my son is asleep and my wife is stifling yawns. Somehow I don't have the heart to make her stay up with me, so after I've had a bath and dinner I end up saying, "Don't worry about me. Why don't you just go to bed?" And so, it's about one o'clock when I start drinking. Listening to FM broadcasts with the volume turned low, under the low ceiling of our apartment in this housing development I drink as I indulge in wild fantasies. At such times moderation just doesn't seem to fill the bill.

I realize that if I could at least think that my first-grader son might be asleep in the next room, my state of mind would be very different. It's been four days now since my wife went to visit her family, and I was wondering how I would get through another five days in an apartment where I couldn't hear my son talking in his sleep or my wife's robust snoring. When I got home from the office with those thoughts on my mind, I was surprised to see you standing in front of the door. It's a relief to hear that my mother-in-law's illness isn't as bad as we thought. Hey, let's drink today. It's been ten years. No, twelve. Twelve years! We're both guilty of not keeping in touch. But I'm glad you came. You seem to be doing well. But that doesn't really matter one way or the other. I'm going to begin with a story I've been saving. But before I do, let's have another drink and wet our whistles.

It was the winter of my sophomore year in college. Let's see, how many years ago would that make it? Hmm, that's four-teen years ago. You remember, don't you, that Dunhill lighter? It was an antique we found in the bottom of my late father's desk when we were going through his belongings. You really wanted it, didn't you? When we polished it with some tooth-paste "Dunhill, Made in England, 1929" became legible. It still worked. You even went to the trouble to go buy some oil and test it. I still remember your face as you said, "It lit!" You gazed at the flame for a long time then grabbed the lighter from my hand and shouted, "Hey, this is really some lighter!"

You said it was priceless. "Nineteen twenty-nine must be the year it was made. I've heard different theories, but at any rate it was in 1921 that Dunhill first made lighters, and those were only prototypes. It probably took a few years before they made full-fledged oil lighters, and those were imported to Japan in 1925, so this is really some lighter. Most of the silver plating has been worn off the brass, but hey, that makes it even better, doesn't it? What's even more important is its shape! There's nothing superfluous about it—if anything it's almost too simple—but it has a dignity about it that says, *this* is a lighter.

"And then there's its lid: round at the base. It's the type that screws on; when you take it off, there's a place specially made in the base to store spare flints. Can you believe this lighter was made fifty-four years ago?" You went on and on like that. Then you glanced up at me and said, "I'll give you ten thousand yen for it." When I answered with silence, you jacked your offer all the way up to fifty thousand yen. Fifty thousand yen! You wanted it so badly that your mouth was watering.

At any rate, my old man died leaving debts, my mom wasn't in good health, I still had two years to finish college, and as if that weren't enough we didn't know where our next meal was coming from. The reason I didn't accept your offer then wasn't because I was obsessed with the price. Nor was I thinking of selling the lighter to a collector who might offer more. I was puzzled about why my old man should treasure an antique lighter like that. He wasn't the sort of man who was given over to such things. Lighting up with a match was fine for him. He was that way about things, and so I sensed that this lighter must have had some special memory for him, something that he couldn't mention to anyone. It was right after his death, and I think I was a bit sentimental.

Ten days after you had given up and gone home, I really wanted the fifty thousand yen. We were besieged by bill collectors, Mom was sick in bed, the house had been mortgaged, and we had to find an apartment somewhere. But Mom and I had already turned everything into cash that could be; we were flat broke. I had no choice but to let you buy the lighter. I should have called you before setting out, but even after scraping together every one- and five-yen coin in the house, there still wasn't enough to place a phone call. There was only enough for a one-way fare from our place in Fukushima Ward to Sakai, where your house was located. It's strange; it really was exactly a one-way fare. When I think about it now, everything seemed to fall into place. You know what I mean? If I had called and told you that I'd sell you the lighter, you'd have come running. But the only thing on my mind then was the five ten thousand-yen bills, and all I could think of was that if I called you, I'd be ten yen short for the train fare. When things aren't going well, that's how everything turns out.

It was after 8:00 p.m. on the fifteenth of February when I got on a bus for Osaka Station, took the subway from there to Namba, then transferred to the Nankai line. After buying my ticket for Sakai, I was flat broke. All I had in my pocket was the lighter to be sold for fifty thousand yen. As I was rocked by the motion of the train, the only thing I could think of was that after getting paid for the lighter, on the way back I'd treat myself to some hot saké at a roasted chicken shop in Umeda.

It was about 9:30 when I arrived at your house. There wasn't a single light on, and there was no response no matter how many times I rang the doorbell. Shivering, I waited nearly an hour in front of that imposing gate with the tiled roof for someone to come home. The dog next door was barking furiously, and I was prepared to stand in front of your house for two or three hours until your neighbor told me that your entire family had left the day before on a tour of Kyushu, so you probably wouldn't return anytime soon. Do you have any idea how I felt at that moment? It wasn't just that everything was getting dark before my eyes. I was penniless. The wind was so strong I thought it would tear my ears off. And what's more, I had had nothing but a glass of milk that morning, and my stomach was empty.

I trudged to the station, thinking that I could explain the situation to the stationmaster and borrow some money. But after my father's death, one incident after another made it painfully clear to me that not everyone in the world had good intentions, and I just couldn't bring myself to open the door to the stationmaster's office.

I looked for a pawnshop. Any pawnshop would be willing to lend money for an item this valuable. I found a sign for a pawnshop on a utility pole and walked in the direction indicated, but on the way I suddenly changed my mind. I was furious at you for having set the price at fifty thousand yen. In those days the starting salary of a new college graduate was only around thirty thousand per month. And there I was heading for a pawnshop with a pathetic look on my face just because I didn't have a measly two hundred yen. "Hah! So your family is off traveling in Kyushu, huh? 'Let me have it for fifty thousand yen,' you say? Damn it, I'll walk home if it kills me!" Such thoughts suddenly crossed my mind.

I went back to the station and for a while followed a road parallel to the tracks. Eventually it came to a dead end. After zigzagging though alleys, I managed to come out on the national highway. "Bone-chilling" describes the cold on a night like that.

Now don't look so disgusted. I'm not voicing resentment or anything like that. I just want to tell you how I walked from Sakai all the way to Fukushima Ward one night in the middle of winter, that's all. One thing occupied my thoughts as I walked along: *I wonder if a patrol car will come along. I hope the policeman in the car will be suspicious of me plodding along by myself in the middle of the night and question me. Then I'll explain everything. And maybe he'll give me a ride home in the patrol car.* But no matter how I tried to walk like a hoodlum or to act like a thief, tripping along and glancing about furtively, no patrol car stopped.

I walked, I guess, for about three hours. No, it was probably only two at most. I had lost all sense of time and direction and like a dead man was beyond the point of feeling cold, so that I could do nothing but plod on ahead. The luminous paint on road signs glistened in the headlights of passing trucks, and I could see the words "Route 26" and "Sumiyoshi Park, 10 kilometers." I realized that I had been walking in the wrong direction and with a groan began retracing my steps.

Route 26 is a straight shot to Namba. "Oh, whatever, I'll just walk along this road." At that thought I felt slightly invigorated. Beyond Sumiyoshi is Kohama, and beyond Kohama is Kishinosato. Beyond that is Hanazono-chō, then Daikoku-chō. After that Namba is only a stone's throw away. After reaching Namba, it would only take an hour-and-a-half or two hours to Fukushima. I drew a mental map, and as I was verifying the place names on it, I panicked. You know what I mean, don't you? At this rate, I'd pass through Hanazono-chō at dawn or shortly before. That's Hanazono-chō, where the day laborer recruiters are located! I'll have to go right through the middle of Hanazono-chō, where there'll surely be several frozen corpses by the road at daybreak on a cold day like this.

My resolve to walk home no matter what wavered. But my feet kept moving mechanically. There wasn't a soul on the street, but the road rumbled with the sound of every passing truck. Before long I had the feeling that I was being followed, and when I looked back there was a man on a bicycle about ten meters behind me, adjusting his speed to my pace and tilting left and right as he pumped the pedals. I stopped to pee in order to let him go past, but then he dismounted and peed. I stealthily picked up a rock the size of a softball, put it in my coat pocket, and kept a grip on it. When I started walking, that guy again got on his bike and followed. I thought of slipping into some alley to get away from him, but since he was on a bicycle he would surely catch up to me. All kinds of things crossed my mind. Who the hell was this guy? A killer? A thief? If he was a thief, he would just take the lighter and that would be that, but if he was out to kill someone, what could I do?

Finally I couldn't stand it any longer, so I turned around and said, "What're you following me for? I don't have one yen on me. Please go away."

I hadn't realized until then that my lips were numb and that I was slobbering. The man didn't say a word but just stared at me for a while and then got off his bike, which he pushed toward me. His face was illuminated by the headlights of a car: I'd say he was about twenty-five or twenty-six, had a buzz cut, thick lips, and eyebrows that were twice as bushy as those of an ordinary person. I was about to scream for help.

"Where're you headed?" When he finally spoke his voice was strangely gentle, like a woman's.

In spite of that, I kept a grip on the rock in my pocket as I answered, "I'm going back to Fukushima."

"Fukushima. You mean Fukushima Ward?"

"That's right."

"Why don't you take the train?"

"Because I don't have any money."

The man tapped the rack of his bike and said, "Hop on! I'll take you there."

You can't just "hop on" because someone says to, you know. I refused his offer, told him to stop following me, and again started walking. No matter how many times I turned and looked back, he was right behind me. This went on until we got to Sumiyoshi Park.

I sat down in front of a weathered old building because my legs were aching and I had even felt dizzy a few times.

"Hop on! I'll take you there." He repeated the same thing six or seven times even though he got no answer from me.

"Where're you planning on taking me once you get me on the back of your bicycle?"

"To Fukushima."

"Liar! I won't fall for that. Like I've been saying all along, I don't have a yen on me. I'm so starved that my nose won't even bleed. No matter how you try to trap me, it won't work. You want to take me to a sweatshop somewhere for cheap labor, don't you?"

"Whaddya mean, a 'sweatshop for cheap labor'?"

I turned up the collar of my coat and crouched down for a long time with my face buried between my knees.

"If you just sit there like that, you'll die. I'll take you where you're headed, so get on." He spoke in a relaxed tone as if trying to calm a fretful child.

I lifted my head and asked, "Don't you have a home?"

"Sure, I have a home."

"Then hurry and go back to it. You don't give up, do you? If you hang around with me, you're the one who will end up dying."

"I want to die," he said with a big smile on his face. It was that smile that broke my resistance. It was a strange smile. I stood up and straddled the rack. In a big voice he said gleefully "We're off!" and began pumping the pedals furiously. "Hang on tight!"

I wrapped my arms around him and was startled: under his thin jacket he was wearing neither a sweater nor any underwear. And it was below freezing that night, I tell you. According to the evening newspapers, it would be the lowest temperature of the year: 20°F in the morning, and it had been four years since the mercury had gone below 22°F in Osaka. The warmth that came through that thin jacket felt good. He was working the pedals just like a pro bike racer. An oddball, to be sure, but he didn't seem like such a bad fellow. *Well, whatever, if he'll really get me to Fukushima, then it's my gain.* With that thought, I warmed my cheeks one after the other against his back. Then an unpleasant premonition came over me because of his one statement: "I want to die." Was he looking for someone to die with him? His wasn't the usual way you'd pump bicycle pedals. Was he really of a mind to die? I frantically tapped him on the back and asked him to slow down.

With surprising acquiescence he did as I requested, and asked, "Are you afraid?"

I told him that my butt hurt and asked, "A while ago you said you wanted to die, didn't you? Why?"

The howling of the wind was stronger than the roar of the trucks on their long-distance routes as they passed by, almost grazing us. We were riding into the wind, and I don't think I'll ever again experience a night as cold as that one. After some time he stopped, turned around and said, "A while ago,

I wanted to die, but now I want to live. About five thousand times a day I want to die and then to live. My brother and the doctors at the hospital say I'm sick, but no matter how I think about it I can't see it as an illness. Isn't everybody like that? How about you?"

I quickly got off the rack. *Why hadn't I caught on sooner? This guy must have a screw loose.* I shuddered when that occurred to me. I thanked him politely. "We're almost to Kishinosato. I'll be okay from there. You've been a big help. Don't take it wrong, but please go on back by yourself." I tried to get away, but as soon as I started walking he followed, this time not behind, but at my side. I made up my mind not to answer him, but he kept talking for all he was worth. Finally, he said something that baffled me.

"You think I'm nuts, don't you? Why? Even you sometimes want to die and sometimes want to live, don't you? It's only human beings who think that way, right? So isn't it just proof that I'm a normal human being?"

When he put it that way, it certainly seemed to make sense. Even though I had resolved not to answer him, in spite of myself I ended up saying, "Well, yes. . . . But in one day to go back and forth five thousand times between wanting to die and wanting to live, that's not normal."

"You think so?" He clammed up and was lost in thought. We could see the signboard and clock of a bank at a large intersection we were approaching. It was three o'clock. "My God, I've been walking nearly five hours, and I still haven't reached Kishinosato!" That thought sapped my energy. My companion was looking at the clock too.

"I know."

"What do you know?"

"It's not just five thousand times that I've died, but more like fifty thousand or five hundred thousand, so many times I could never count them. I understand that very clearly the moment I start having a keen desire to live. On the other

hand, when I want to die, I'm completely unable to recall anything before I was born. I lose my sense of having been reborn
countless times."

I again straddled the rack and said in a languid voice,
"Please, take me to Fukushima. I don't have the energy to walk
any further. But let me know if you start wanting to die. That
way I can jump off the rack."

He let out a laugh. No matter how I looked at his face, it
didn't seem like the face of a person with a screw loose. And
yet when I thought about it, anyone who would offer a total
stranger a ride on his bicycle in the middle of the night as far as
Fukushima certainly *is* odd. My willingness to keep company
with an oddball like him probably showed the depths to which
I had fallen.

We started moving at a hair-raising speed. Not five minutes had passed when he shouted, "Hey, I've started wanting to
die!" I jumped off. It was right in the middle of an intersection.
He rode across the intersection and stopped, his head drooping and motionless.

"I'm going to walk until you want to live," I said as I hurried
down the sidewalk past a row of houses. Without moving a
muscle he sat astride his bicycle, his head drooping. After I
had walked a fair distance and left him behind in the dark, a
light the size of a bean grew stronger as it approached. It was
the light on his bicycle.

"Hey, it's okay. Hop on!"

"No kidding? Hey, take it easy. Until that odd fit of yours
completely subsides, there's no way I'm getting on that bicycle!"

"I'm in an incredibly happy mood. No matter how many
times you die, you'll be reborn. As long as you know that, how
can you be afraid of anything in this world? Hop on!"

How many times do you think that guy shouted "I want to
die" before we got to Hanazono-chō? It wasn't just ten or twenty times. Each time I would frantically jump off, and I don't

know how many times I jumped awkwardly and fell down. As the wind subsided, the temperature dropped. My body was like ice, but something had been born in my heart that warmed it. It wasn't the fact that some passing oddball had performed an act of kindness. When he wanted to live again and said with a gleam in his eyes "No matter how many times you die, you'll be reborn," I felt happy too, and every time he said it I responded in all seriousness, "Really? That's good."

Just as the sky was beginning to show a tinge of blue, we approached the area under the Hanazono-chō overpass. From the rack where I was seated I said, "Hey, there are always a lot of troublemakers hanging around here, so don't start wanting to die."

"It doesn't do any good to say that. It can happen anywhere."

There they were: in workman's split-toed shoes with torn-in-half cigarettes behind their ears, wrapped in newspapers and lying by the side of the road. We couldn't be certain whether were dead or just asleep. I prayed that this oddball wouldn't start wanting to die. Several men emerged from the shadows of houses and alleys, cheeks hollow and faces earthen-colored.

"Hey, go faster."

No sooner had I said that than more than a dozen of them were surrounding the bicycle. Noticing the gathering, a lot of other ominous-looking types also assembled and started to say things like: "What is it? Have they got work?" "Hey, where are these guys from?" I felt more dead than alive. We were surrounded by a crowd of at least fifty, all anxious to find work as soon as possible. The oddball nodded to several of them in a friendly manner and said, "Good morning!" With a greeting like that, you look like someone who's come with an offer of work. They all clamored to grab onto the handlebars or seat of the bicycle.

"Is it one or two people that you need?"

"Hey, I was first! Sir, none of these guys are fit enough to last until noon. I'm the only one who can keep at it until quitting time."

I thought we were done for. As soon as those guys realized that we were just passing through they wouldn't just let it go at that. They'd be furious and would give us both a good trouncing. And even if we tried to escape there would be no way we could with all of them surrounding the bicycle and holding on to it. The oddball just kept repeating like an idiot, "Good morning! Good morning!" Then suddenly he said, "All of you, follow me!"

The man missing both front teeth who was standing directly in front with both hands on the handlebars asked, "All of us? What kind of work have you got for all of us?"

"Never mind. Just let us through and then follow us. It's work that all of you can do."

The man signaled to open a path for us.

"Can you use old men too?" A voice came from behind the crowd.

"It's not the sort of work that requires physical strength, so old men are fine." He motioned for everyone to follow and began slowly pumping the bicycle pedals. We went under the overpass and proceeded onto the road to Daikoku-chō at a leisurely pace, followed by a crowd of more than seventy workers who were saying to each other in low voices, "What sort of work is it?" "I've never seen these recruiters before."

I leaned close to the oddball's ear and said, "Go! Now!" But he didn't increase his speed. I suddenly wondered what state of mind he was in. Did he want to die? Did he want to live? Feeling the stares of scores of men on my back, I asked, "Hey, do you want to die now? Or to live?"

"Neither."

"You have times like that too?"

"It's been three years now since I felt this way. Until three years ago, I didn't care one way or the other."

I poked him in the back and told him to look behind us. "What do you think these guys have in mind? If we don't get out of here fast, we're in for it."

"If we run now, they'll catch us right away."

He was right. Even after we had gone under the overpass, the street was lined on both sides for a good distance with huddled men waiting for a recruiter's car to show up. I looked blankly at the faceless crowd parading behind us along the frozen road in the dawn. A parade is what they were. The sound of the first passing train reverberated above the overpass. There were few people loitering on the sidewalks or in the street. Just as we started going downhill, he accelerated. I didn't care whether he wanted to live or die.

"I'll die with you! Go! As fast as you can!" I was shouting. A car coming from a side street slammed on its brakes. The street must have been icy in places because at the corner the car slid into a stall selling roast giblets. Several of the unemployed day laborers were in hot pursuit, and two or three of them were throwing rocks at us. I saw one of them slip and fall as he threw a rock. We were racing away at breakneck speed.

We sped through a street in Daikokuo-chō lined with shoe stores, past a street in Namba full of "love hotels" with neon lights ablaze and crossed the Minato-machi district into the Yotsubashi area. During that time how many times do you suppose that guy shouted, "I've started wanting to die!"?

Each time, I wrapped my arms around him, gave him a squeeze, and said, "Don't worry. I'll die with you."

We arrived near my home in Fukushima Ward about the time workers were hurrying to train stations, their breath white in the frosty air.

I got off the bicycle and thanked him. His thin jacket was soaked with perspiration. I insisted that he take it off and gave him my own coat. I told him how to get back without going through Hanazono-chō, but, whether he was really listening or not, he didn't seem to understand. No matter how I turn that image around in my mind as I recall his face bathed in the morning sunlight, there is no more apt word to describe it than "divine." My coat was a bit small for him, but I felt deeply obliged as I thanked him. I wanted to do something more for him but didn't have the money to buy even a single bean-jam bun. He waved and then came back after going several yards.

"Do you think I'm sick?" he asked.

I wasn't able to answer. I could neither nod nor shake my head. He kept waiting for me to say something. Since I couldn't very well remain silent, I responded with a question. "Do you really think you've died countless times?"

I'll never forget the pity that filled his eyes as he said with a disappointed look on his face, "Why can't you understand that?" Then he gently stroked my head.

Three days after that, my mother and I moved out of our house and into an apartment in Yodogawa Ward.

I've never told this story to anyone. I've been saving it. Don't pull such a strange face. You probably think I've just taken up a lot of your time telling you a pointless tale. You want me to get to the point, don't you? I knew from the beginning why you took the trouble to come from Osaka to Tokyo and search out the housing project where I live. It's the lighter, isn't it? The Dunhill oil lighter. It was in the pocket of my coat, the coat I gave to the guy with the buzz cut who wanted to live and die five thousand times a day.

The Stairs

階段

I NEVER AGAIN WANT to set foot in an apartment building where poor people live. It scares me just to pass close to such a place.

Nowadays even if one walks down a back street in a large city, two-story rental houses are lined up next to buildings with names ending in "suites" in spite of the stains that cling to their filthy walls in icicle-like patterns. But back in 1962 or 1963 when I was in high school, any place you went was crowded with wretched-looking apartments, their roofs of tin or poor-quality mortar, the cracks in their windows pasted over with paper cut in cherry blossom patterns.

In such apartments, the odor of all manner of human excreta always hung in the air. The wailing of infants and the coughing of old people could be heard, and empty saké and soy sauce bottles littered the dusty, dingy hallways and stairways. Most of the children were snot-nosed, and for whatever reason there would always be one or two occupants who were not quite in their right minds.

Our family was living in the S district of Osaka's Taishō Ward at the time. In an alley off the road where the streetcar ran wooden-frame apartment buildings closely surrounded dilapidated houses unfit for habitation, their rooflines heaving and sinking, their front doors broken or missing. Our family moved five times in only two years, and about the time I started high school we ended up in Kamei Manor.

Six months before, Dad had seriously injured Mom and then disappeared, never to be heard from again. It all started with some minor complaint Mom made. Dad, who had never before even raised his voice, picked up a teapot and threw it at Mom. The teapot hit her head and broke, inflicting a seven-centimeter gash by her temple. The deepest part of the wound went to the bone, and perhaps that was why even after it healed she was tormented by persistent headaches.

On April 15, 1962 Mom, my older brother and I moved into a west-facing apartment consisting of one six-mat room on the second floor of Kamei Manor. The reason I remember the date is because it was Mom's birthday. And it was the day when Mom, who until then had never drunk a drop of liquor except on New Year's, imbibed a mere cup of second-grade saké, which eventually led to hellish days.

On the day we were forced by circumstances to move there, my brother had already decided to quit high school in his senior year and take a job at an electronic parts factory in Sakai.

"Dad'll never come back. He's such a coward that he thinks the cops are still after him for hurting Mom. He'll run around on the lam and then probably hang himself somewhere," my brother said as we hauled a chest of drawers up the narrow, steep steps of Kamei Manor. He rubbed his upper lip where he was sporting a thickening moustache. Once we had placed the chest of drawers in front of the wall facing the hallway, our move was complete, and my brother got ready to go to the factory dormitory. He had been studious and left behind several reference books for me. He gave Mom half of the moving allowance he had received from the factory. "Mom, when your head aches, you ought to try drinking a bit of saké," he said. "Besides, it's your birthday. Let's celebrate that and my new job."

Since elementary school my brother had gotten good grades. In high school he would study every night until one o'clock unless something important came up. He was the sort who seldom showed his feelings, but that day he was unusually talkative, and the jolliness that so poorly suited him made Mom and me more taciturn than ever. He had to be in the dormitory next to the factory by nine o'clock that night, but he showed no sign of leaving even though it was past seven. He planted a five-hundred-yen bill in my hand and told me to go buy something.

"There's a liquor store on the other side of the streetcar stop, isn't there? Go pick out something you think would be good."

In spite of being worried that my brother might not make it to the dormitory before curfew, I took my time going down the muddy stairs of Kamei Manor. Here and there lay the rusty remains of children's tricycles, and a voice could be heard chanting a sutra to the accompaniment of wooden clappers. Kamei Manor had its own peculiar stench. And the Kikuya Apartments next door and the Matsuba Manor across the alley each had their own peculiar stench that enveloped their tenants day and night, depriving them of all hope, draining them of strength, provoking anger, and turning their energy into irritability and despair.

At the liquor store, which also had a standing bar, I threaded my way through the crowd, selected some boiled fish paste and dried globefish, bought a pint of second-rate saké, and returned to Kamei Manor. Mom seemed to have been crying while I was away. There were traces of tears on my brother's cheeks too, but as I handed the change to him I cried out, "Cheers, cheers!" I was afraid of being told that I should quit high school too and go to work. My grades were no comparison to his, but when he decided to get a job, I resolved that I would study hard and show everyone that I could get into a national university.

My brother broke the seal on the pint bottle and urged Mom to have some.

"Won't it just make my headache worse?" After hesitating, she drank a bit. Having made sure that she had, my brother stood up and, insisting that there was no need for us to see him off, took his bag and left. Now that I think about it he, too, probably wanted to get far away from the stench of apartments where poor people live and from the unhappiness that unfolds in such places. My brother never again set foot in Kamei Manor, and we have an unwritten agreement never to mention the night we moved into the place. But he only knows about the incidents involving Mom and has no way of knowing how I responded.

Only after she had timidly sipped a cup and a half from a somewhat larger teacup did Mom realize that the saké that went to her stomach cured her headache.

"I'd heard that saké was a cure-all, but, really, that persistent headache has vanished as if I never had it. But if I drink more than this, it'll make my heart race." With that Mom set about fixing my dinner, setting the rice cooker next to the sink, taking the dishes out of the cardboard boxes, and beginning to wash them. But within a week, that cup of saké had made Mom an alcoholic.

THERE WERE SEVEN APARTMENTS in Kamei Manor: three on the first floor and four on the second. Immediately to the right in the entranceway were the mailboxes, and just behind them were the stairs to the second floor. For some reason, there was a small window in the middle of the stairwell. It was at about knee-level for an adult ascending the stairs; so not only did it serve no purpose as a window, but during the summer it focused the setting sun on the linoleum covering the steps, burning and warping it. During the winter a cold draft came through the window, incessantly rattling the room of the young couple who worked at a pachinko parlor.

During the two years and three months we lived there, I don't know how many times I sat down in the middle of those stairs hugging my knees. There were fourteen steps in the staircase. Sitting right in the middle—seven steps from the top, seven from the bottom. From the small window I could see the main road beyond the path between the apartment and a dry cleaner's. The path was paved with boards that covered a gutter and was only wide enough for one person to pass through at a time. I could also peer into the standing bar at the liquor store.

I always sat on the seventh step because if I sat one step higher, through a gap resulting from a poorly installed door I would be visible from the room of the couple from the pachinko parlor. And if I sat one step lower, tenants going in and out of the entranceway would be able to see me.

Yet whenever I recall myself between the spring of my fifteenth and the summer of my seventeenth years sitting in the middle of the stairs in Kamei Manor, I can't help feeling that those weren't the only reasons I sat in that particular spot. Adamantly, as if observing some magical rite, I continued to sit on the same step. It was an unsettling, dirty place, but it was central for getting a sense of what was going on in and around the apartment building. If I focused my attention, I could catch the voices of people who had just gotten off the streetcar or even the feverish, carnal sensation of a couple whispering to each other in the alley. Perhaps by insisting doggedly on that particular step I was desperately attempting to maintain some kind of balance within myself. Even if the seesaw I was riding tilted to one extreme, as long as I sat there motionlessly, I had a stable center.

A fifty-ish man lived alone in the room across the hall from ours. He was not on particularly bad terms with his wife and children, and they were not in financial straits. But for some reason he chose to live apart from them. According to rumors that circulated among the tenants, his wife managed a small pub in Hiroshima, and he would take three days at the end of every month to go be with his family. For the present purposes, I'll call him Shimada Ichirō.

Shimada was short but broad-shouldered, and he walked a bit bandy-legged. He was neither friendly nor unfriendly. Ever since the war had ended he had been working the night shift at a warehouse company near Osaka Harbor. He always left at nine in the evening and returned at seven the next morning. He never drank or went out to eat but would scrupulously fix his own meals in his carefully cleaned room. He even prepared his own box lunches.

Perhaps it was because Shimada lived alone and tended to be a man's man that, except for old men and young boys, the guys who lived in Kamei Manor would often visit his room to watch television or play cards for low stakes.

Among Shimada's nightly visitors was a taxi driver who lived on the first floor, the son of the elderly couple who chanted the Heart Sutra to the accompaniment of wooden clappers. Another was a stage magician who lived in the room next to ours and who, even when Shimada was at work, would not hesitate to unlock his door and go in, lolling on the tatami watching television until late at night. This magician was seldom able to come by any work; three or four days a month performing during intermissions at strip joints was the extent of his employment. Aside from that, he would cadge money from his sister who lived with him and frequent mah-jongg parlors. She was a taciturn, plain young woman who worked in a department store in Shinsaibashi. Some of the scandal-mongering womenfolk in Kamei Manor would say jokingly, "Brother and sister? Yeah, sure!"

But I never doubted that they were siblings. The morning after we moved in, through the wall I overheard her say, "Stop going to play mah-jongg. Everyone already thinks you're a con artist because you're a magician. Are you listening to me?"

"Yeah, I hear you. But if I were enough of a magician to dupe people in my main business of gambling, would I have to rely on my little sister's low wages?"

It was this magician who, bounding up the stairs with deliberate noise, informed me with a slight grin that Mom had brought the streetcar to a stop by falling on the rails and shrieking.

At first, I didn't understand what the magician was talking about. "Hey," he said, "your mother has stopped the streetcar with her legs wide apart. It's quite a scene!" But he was laughing as if it were amusing, and the expression on his face didn't match what he was saying. That day, after coming home from school, I was waiting for Mom to return from applying for work at a confectioner's shop that an acquaintance had recommended.

"She's stopped the streetcar. If you don't hurry and bring her home, drunkards will start fondling her here." The magician tapped his crotch two or three times. With no idea what had happened to Mom, I dashed out of the room and down the stairs. On the way, my knees began to shake. I thought for sure that she must have been run over by the streetcar. Thinking to take a shortcut, I ran through the alley with the covered gutter to the side of the dry cleaner's. Just as I was about to dash out onto the main road I was overwhelmed by the din of cars honking, the commotion of bystanders, and the streetcar's horn. With her skirt pulled up to her waist, Mom was repeating the same slurred words over and over to the streetcar driver and conductor who were trying to get her off the rails, "Go ahead and run over me. Hurry up and run over me!"

I stepped back, hiding behind the crowd of bystanders and making myself inconspicuous on the path over the covered gutter, and watched Mom be carried to the sidewalk by several men. The lights from the liquor store illumined the blue veins up Mom's thighs as she sat on the sidewalk, her head swaying.

"Where do you live, ma'am?" some men, probably laborers, asked Mom when the streetcar started moving and the by-standers began to disperse. At that point, I finally emerged from the shadows of the alley, crossed the street, and went up to her.

"Mom, Mom," I repeated in a small voice as I helped her up so I could take her home.

The liquor store owner thundered at me, "Hey! You caused everyone a lot of trouble. Aren't you going to apologize?"

AFTER REPEATEDLY TELLING ME she was sorry, Mom slipped into the futon I had laid out for her and slept until morning.

I thought that Mom's sudden derangement might have been a transient phenomenon, but that wasn't the case. From that day on, she had to have saké, no matter what, even if it meant no money for food. Her excuse was that if she drank, her head-aches would go away, and if they didn't go away, she wouldn't be able to work. Yet no job she landed ever lasted more than ten days. A forty-three year old woman whose breath reeked of saké by midday and whose speech was slurred would im-mediately be fired no matter where she went.

Mom was constantly on my mind while I was at school—whether during class or breaks. I didn't want to see her drunk. Whenever I had to go pick her up from the streetcar rails, my feelings went beyond bitterness and sadness to the point that my nerves were pretty much numbed. If I hadn't desensitized my nerves, I would never have been able to venture out of the apartment to bring her back when she was writhing on the rails with her skirt pulled up.

I don't know how much money my brother was making then, but I have no doubt that the eight thousand yen he sent us every month was the most he could manage. At any rate, it was 1962, and as a high school dropout he would have been put in the pay category of a middle school graduate.

For rather a long time—well, actually only three weeks—I kept Mom's alcoholism a secret from my brother. But the night after she performed her disgraceful stunt of stopping the streetcar for the fifth time, I couldn't take it any longer and phoned the dormitory where he lived. I'll never forget the silence on the other end of the line. After I explained the situation in detail, he didn't utter a single word. I thought maybe we had been disconnected and shouted "Hello, are you there?"

He just said, "I can't do any more than I'm already doing." With that, he hung up.

In a state of confusion I wandered aimlessly about the nighttime alleys. Suddenly, an idea came to me, and I ran to the liquor store where I asked the owner not to sell her any saké when she came by.

"If she has money, I'll sell it to her. That's my business."

His words infuriated me, and I shot back, "Well then, if she stops the streetcar, don't complain that she's causing trouble for your store!" The owner and one of his employees grabbed me by the collar, dragged me to a nearby vacant lot, and beat me until the inside of my mouth was cut to pieces. For the next three days, I couldn't hear out of my left ear.

There was nothing I could do other than stay home from school and keep a constant watch on Mom. My habit of sitting on the stairs began the first day I cut school to keep her from drinking. Leaning against the wooden frame of the small window and hugging my knees, out of all the sounds in the building I attempted to catch only those that came from our room, which was directly above where I was sitting: the sound of Mom's turning on the faucet, of her leaning against a wall, of her clothing dragging on the tatami. No matter how slight the sound, I was able to tell whether it came from our room or some other room. Eventually, there were no more sounds from our room.

I stealthily got up, climbed to the second floor, and peered into the room. Mom was asleep. Relieved, I locked the door just to make sure and was about to return to my position on the stairs. Shimada came out of his room and asked, "What? You're cutting classes?" Then he whispered, "That kind of illness won't be cured unless you put her in the hospital."

I said I thought alcoholism could be cured by not having any liquor for five days.

Shaking his head with regret, he said, "Even if they stay away from it for ten years, just one drop and it's all over. I have to go take a shit. Go watch TV in my room."

Shimada went to the communal restroom at the end of the hall. I entered his room and sat in front of the television set, next to which was a closet. Its sliding door was slightly ajar, and I peered inside. Bedding was piled up on the top shelf, and two cardboard boxes were sitting on the bottom. One was crammed full of magazines. They were all face down, so I picked one up and took a look at its cover: *The Adventure Club*. Drawings and photos of bound women hanging from trees or chained and wearing collars leaped off the page. With my heart pounding and my ears straining to catch any sound from the direction of the restroom, I flipped through the pages. When I nervously returned the magazine to its original place, I noticed in the other box a thick envelope underneath cigarettes, notebooks, and a memorandum book. Even now I can't explain how, without looking inside, I could tell that it contained scores of banknotes. My mind went blank after being completely absorbed by those two things in Shimada's closet: the lurid magazines that strangely numbed me, and the money.

When Shimada returned, he said, "Why don't you try going to the Public Health Department for advice? Or better yet, the ward office. Well, whichever. Your mother's alcoholism isn't going to be cured if she stays here." Then he rummaged about in his closet, produced a bag of candy, and offered me a piece. I gave a vague answer and popped the candy in my mouth.

"Is it okay if I come by and watch TV once in a while?" I already intended to steal the money.

"My room's like a meeting place." Shimada said laughing as he shut the closet.

During the three days I stayed home from school, Mom didn't drink any saké. Clasping my hand she swore again and again that she would never have another drink. Only four hundred yen remained of what my brother had sent, and his next payday was still ten days away. But that night, Mom took the four hundred yen and bought saké. When I got home from school, she was groaning, "I want to die, I want to die." She stuck her tongue out when she saw me.

"Why are you sticking your tongue out?" I yelled and hit her. Again and again, as hard as I could, I hit my own mother.

After that, I ran out of the room to the middle of the stairs, counting aloud as I descended, and sat down by the small window. Returning from somewhere or other, the magician glanced at me and proceeded up the steps, obviously in a foul mood. He said to Shimada, "The streetcar hasn't been stopped these two or three days."

"That's because her son has been keeping watch."

I called to mind our family's life before Dad absconded. He had managed a small factory that made work gloves. The downturn began when he became the guarantor for a loan to a long-time employee who wanted to go into business for himself. By the time I was in middle school Dad had to sell off the factory and go out to find work. He was by nature querulous and timid, but he neither drank nor gambled. Perhaps because his simple and honest personality was better suited to being a salaried worker than to the stress of managing a small factory, he voiced no particular discontent, and many days passed with his leaving and coming home at fixed times.

Mom was an expert at putting aside secret savings. She had a much better way with words than Dad and a stronger will than her outward manner would lead anyone to believe. Even when Dad had to relinquish the factory, she encouraged all of us saying, "When the right opportunity comes along, he'll be able to have an even bigger factory."

No matter how we had fallen to our present situation, to my fifteen-year-old self it all seemed like a comical dream. How was Dad making a living? And where? Why couldn't Mom quit drinking? But even as I absentmindedly engaged in such thoughts, my attention was focused on the second story.

The magician had retreated to his own room, and Shimada was watching television. If I acted quickly, it could be done in one minute. By the time Shimada got back from the restroom, I could steal the money and be out of the apartment building. But during that one minute, someone might look out into the hallway, or perhaps the magician might come to Shimada's room. If I were caught, how would it all end up? At that time, I didn't give much thought to the deed I was about to commit.

About twenty minutes later, footsteps that were unmistakably Shimada's echoed toward the restroom. I climbed up a few steps and peered down the hallway. Having ascertained that Shimada had gone into the restroom, I checked the door to the magician's apartment. Then I slipped into Shimada's room, opened the closet, lifted up the cigarettes, notebooks, and memorandum book, took out the envelope containing the money, and quickly removed one ten-thousand-yen bill. I then replaced everything, shut the closet door, went out into the hallway, and descended the stairs. I decided not to leave the apartment building and instead sat down in the middle of the stairs because I saw someone's shadow beyond the entranceway door. But whoever it was passed the dry cleaner's and didn't enter Kamei Manor. When Shimada returned from the restroom and called to me from above, my blood instantly froze.

"What's the matter that you're sitting in a place like that?"

I turned around and looked him straight in the face. "I can see the liquor store from here."

"So, you intend to keep watch there all the time?"

I nodded silently with an expression as if to say "Don't you feel sorry for me?" Shimada's swarthy face flashed a smile in response, and he went into his room.

Though my heart was pounding a bit, I was cooler about having stolen Shimada's money than I thought I would be. But I must have been nervous after all; I had sat down one step higher than usual, and that's why Shimada had been able to see my head when he was about to go into his room.

Once a month—sometimes twice—I would sneak into Shimada's room and steal money. Upon returning from school I would sit on the stairs by the small window and, pricking up my ears, wait for a minute when there was no one in the hallway. Sometimes I would go more than three months without finding that right minute. And sometimes my resolve would break through my indecisiveness and I would stand up only to have the magician or a member of the family down the hall emerge from their rooms.

Mom kept drowning herself in alcohol, and each time I would beat her. How many times did she take my hand and swear that she wouldn't drink again? But it was never more than five days until she would be making a disgrace of herself on the streetcar rails, at the entrance to the marketplace, or in the alley lined with apartment buildings.

I stole 85,000 yen from Shimada. Eight months after I began stealing, he changed the lock on his door. He must have thought the money was being stolen while he was away at work. I thought it strange that he went eight months without noticing the missing money, but I thought it even stranger that no one caught on to my theft.

The day Shimada had the lock changed, I decided that I would no longer slip into his room, and I kept that resolution. But except for cold winter days, I continued to sit in the middle of the stairs. Shimada moved out of Kamei Manor. The magician left one day and never returned. Eventually his sister likewise disappeared, and new tenants moved in. But when I got home from school I continued to sit on the stairs, all ears, listening to every sound in the smelly apartment building: the sound of people rinsing their mouths or turning over in their sleep, the sound of bedding being laid out, the sound of a spoon stirring instant coffee, the sound of Mom tapping the tatami when she wanted to drink some saké.

At some point, I became attuned to sounds outside the building as well, and my mind began to search for more distant sounds, sounds that were really inaudible. Those were sounds that I made up myself. Yet whenever I indulged in such auditory fantasies, from far beyond I could hear myself hitting Mom.

About the time I got married at age twenty-four, Mom suffered from a heart ailment and was no longer able to drink. Her highly irregular pulse would go wild with even a small amount of liquor, and she was barely able to breathe, so she quit drinking. She had no choice really. Dad never showed up again, and even now, we have no idea where he is. By attending high school at night my brother was able to graduate, after which he got a job at a pharmaceutical company. He now lives in Nagoya and is the father of three daughters.

Most of the time I never think about it, but spurred by something or other I sometimes recall my feelings as I sat on the stairs in Kamei Manor. I feel heavy-hearted, and my palms break out in a cold sweat. I'm overcome with fright when I think of what would have happened if my thievery had come to light, and all of the sounds I heard turn into one question that draws me back to the middle of the stairs, "Why were you protected? Why was someone like you protected, someone who would strike his own mother whatever the cause may have been?" And that question causes me to hang my head before eventually rising to my feet.

Vengeance

復讐

CLASSES HAD ALREADY BEGUN, but the three of us were forced to remain in formal sitting position on the floor in the middle of the judo drill hall.

Tsugawa's nosebleed had stopped, but he was not even permitted to wipe the drying blood around his nostrils, lips, chin, and chest. In his earthen-colored face, all that retained natural color were his freckles.

Mitsuoka's right cheek was swollen, and a welt shaped like three fingers had risen. I was the only one who hadn't been beaten, but I had been swept over the teacher's hip and slammed down in the drill hall five times in succession until I could hardly stand up. Even in formal sitting position I couldn't stop my upper body from swaying.

Kamisaka, the gym teacher and also the coach of the judo club, spoke as he walked back and forth in front of us in his burgundy-colored training outfit. "Sit there like that until tomorrow morning! If you make the slightest move, I'll squash your eyeballs, rupture your eardrums, and knock your teeth out."

We knew very well that was no empty threat. I felt as if I were about to cry, and trembled as I suppressed my tears.

"It's clearly written at the entrance: you can't just come into the drill hall any time you please. And yet, knowing that, you imitate pro wrestlers in the sacred space of this Meitoku Hall. That's proof enough that you have no respect for me."

Kamisaka went into the equipment room on his short legs and came back carrying in one hand a fifty-kilo barbell, which he placed gently on the plastic sheet covering the tatami. His upper body was like the gnarled root of an enormous tree. He had graduated from a college in Kansai that produced famous judo champions and had taken first place four years straight in league competition. His face seemed somehow out of proportion with its thick lips and bulging eyes. Behind his back we called him "Idiot Shorty." Sitting down on the bar of the barbell, Kamisaka said, "The blood's no longer circulating in your toes. In a couple more hours they'll start to rot, and after five hours the skin on the top of your feet will rot and peel off."

After sitting in formal position for forty minutes, both of my feet felt as if they were already beginning to rot, whether because of the sitting position or because of fear. From the back pocket of his training outfit Kamisaka produced a crumpled pack of cigarettes and a pornographic photo and held them before us.

"The cigarettes are yours, Mitsuoka. And this piss-smelling picture is yours, Tsugawa. Am I right?" Both Tsugawa and Mitsuoka nodded weakly. Kamisaka fixed his eyes on me and screwed up his thin lips.

"You share the blame, too, because you three are pals. You smoked, too, didn't you? If you can't honestly say 'Yes, I smoked,' then just for you I could teach a special lesson in judo now."

Then he stood up. I promptly answered in a hollow voice, "Yes, I smoked."

"Don't move!" He thundered at me as my torso dizzily rocked in all directions. He again sat down on the bar of the barbell. "If you don't like the way I do things, tell your parents and have them file a police report, but you'll just end up getting booted out of this school, too."

Kamisaka gave a barely audible laugh. Ours was a private high school for boys. We had gotten a new principal over the summer break, and beginning with the second semester the troublemakers had been mercilessly expelled. Mitsuoka proved tough in fights, but his grades were good and he was hoping to get into a national university. I realized that Kamisaka's target was Mitsuoka. Right around the beginning of the new semester, Mitsuoka had gotten into a fight with the captain of the judo club and, to the cheers of well over a hundred pupils forming a circle around them in a corner of the schoolyard, trounced his opponent so soundly that he wasn't able to get up.

Kamisaka fixed his bulging eyes on Mitsuoka. "Hey, Mitsuoka, if you can beat me, you can leave this drill hall, and take them with you." Tsugawa and I stole sideward glances at each other, holding our breaths as we wondered what Mitsuoka would do. Mitsuoka's eyes had become bloodshot. But, remaining in formal sitting posture, he held his tongue.

Two hours later, Kamisaka slapped each of us and allowed us to leave. A metallic ringing in my ears lasted for the longest time. After classes, our homeroom teacher called the three of us to the faculty room and interrogated us as to our whereabouts during the three hours of classes we had missed. We didn't breathe a word about the incident at the Meitoku Hall. We just said that while we were horsing around during the noon break, we got into a fight, and then went up to the rooftop to cool the swelling. Because of Tsugawa's nose and the swelling in Mitsuoka's and my cheeks, we got off with a severe reprimand. While we were being bawled out, Kamisaka sat at his desk nearby and said over and over as if wanting to be overheard, "Ah, this body of mine's becoming worthless!"

That evening on the way to the station, Mitsuoka said with his eyes cast to the ground like a drunkard, "I swear, I'm gonna kill that jerk! He's no schoolteacher, he's a thug. I'm gonna kill him."

"Get real! You'd just end up getting killed yourself. You saw, didn't you, how he could lift a fifty-kilo barbell with just one hand?" Tsugawa said as he sighed and covered his nose with a handkerchief.

With my hands against my still-numb waist I said, "I really thought my legs would rot. By stuffing cigarettes and porn in your pockets, you two gave him license to do as he pleased. Since the end of summer vacation, there've already been six expulsions from this school. Even he thought he had gone too far, and he tried to justify himself by setting the cigarettes and porn in front of us like that."

After Tsugawa and I got on the train, Mitsuoka remained motionless on the bench in the station.

For two or three days after that, I was filled with unbearable indignation and wanted to bring that empty-headed gym teacher to some mortifying shame. But as the days passed, it gradually became engraved in my memory as what would eventually be an odd and somewhat comical recollection from my high school years. One month later, Mitsuoka and Tsugawa were called out of class by the teacher in charge of student conduct and never returned.

AFTER GRADUATING FROM COLLEGE, I was employed in Osaka at the headquarters of a pharmaceutical company. The day after I got my winter bonus, I worked overtime until late and trudged wearily out of the office. Three years had passed since I had started working there. But my bonus money wouldn't cover the debts I had racked up with the bookies at the racetracks.

Someone called my name as I was going through the central entrance of Osaka Station. A man wearing a brown, iridescent, Japanese-style coat, white *tabi* socks, and new sandals said with a faint smile, "Been awhile, hasn't it?" From head to toe his was more of a gangster's appearance than you would see in any movie. Four henchmen stood by him, two in front and two in back.

I panicked and drew back, thinking for sure he was a debt collector from one of the bookies.

"It's me, it's me. Mitsuoka," the man said, his folded arms inserted into the opposite sleeves of his coat.

"Mitsuoka?"

"How soon you forget! Well, you're the only one who finished high school, graduated from college, and now works for a first-rate firm."

No doubt about it; it was Mitsuoka. I hadn't seen him since the day he left the classroom.

"Working this late? What dedication!"

I gingerly stepped up to him and said in a low voice, "It's been a long time. How are you?" Then, out of a feeling of both relief and familiarity, I added without thinking, "You look quite the gangster, don't you?" After letting that out, I thought, *Damn*!

But Mitsuoka, smiling magnanimously, just clicked his tongue and, reproving his henchmen who were glaring at me, extended an invitation. "Are you busy now? If you're free, I'll buy you a drink."

Glancing at the overly polished shoes and double-breasted coats of his henchmen, I responded in an ambivalent tone, "I don't have any particular plans. . . ."

Mitsuoka again smiled slightly, then turned to his henchmen and, as if shooing away dogs, said, "All of you leave! A proper gentleman like him can't drink in peace with guys like you hanging around. Except for the driver, all of you leave!"

A white Lincoln was parked in front of the central entrance. As soon as the henchman-driver saw Mitsuoka he nimbly opened the backseat door. No sooner had it closed than the other henchmen said, bowing and in unison, "Please excuse us, then." Then they all disappeared in the direction of the taxi stands.

"How about Ulysses? We haven't gone there for a while."

"I hear that Maruchō's there today."

"Hmm, Maruchō . . . I don't really need to meet with that old fool."

"Those three have been asked to wait tonight. What would you like to do about them?"

"Those three? . . . Oh, yes! Where are they?"

The driver held up his little finger.

"Okay, I guess it can't be helped. Go there, then."

Listening to the conversation between Mitsuoka and his henchman-driver, I wanted to get out of the car. But the white Lincoln had already left New Midōsuji Boulevard and was on the main Midōsuji Boulevard, almost as far already as Honmachi.

"There was a guy who looked a lot like you standing at the Sakurabashi intersection, so I had the car slow down to match your pace. Didn't you notice?" Mitsuoka put his arm around my shoulder.

I said I hadn't noticed, and asked, "What's Tsugawa up to these days?" There was nothing else we could talk about. What I really wanted to know was how Mitsuoka, the second son of a fusuma maker, after being expelled from high school ended up in this underworld where, at only twenty-five, he was sitting in lordly fashion in the back seat of a Lincoln with several henchmen at his beck and call. But it would take a lot of guts to ask about that, and I thought it best not to pry into such matters.

"He has a shop for grilled tripe in Tanimachi. He more or less took it over from his old man." Then, offering me a cigarette, he whispered to me, "Tsugawa still holds a grudge. I was the one who said I'd kill Idiot Shorty, but now it's Tsugawa who brings that up every time I run into him. He bore a grudge against you, too, Nagai, and pointed out that after we were expelled, you never so much as phoned, even though the three of us had always been buddies."

"After that, I was called in by our homeroom teacher and told that if I was ever caught hanging around with you two, I'd be expelled also."

Mitsuoka made several slight nods and said, "Oh, I see. If you were expelled, you wouldn't have been able to go to college." I wasn't able to tell what he was really thinking, since he now inhabited a world completely different from mine. I sensed that perhaps, employing the methods of that world, he intended to get even with me since I had broken off relations with them and was afraid of getting involved.

"So, Nagai, are you married?"

"No, still a bachelor. I haven't had time for anything like marriage." I left it at that, but just thinking about how much I owed the bookies made my palms sweat.

The conspicuous foreign car honked its way through the congestion on Midōsuji Boulevard and, upon entering the Sōemon district, turned left and right through one-way streets in the red-light district before stopping in front of a club named Perion. A young man standing in the entranceway hurriedly opened the car door. The entrance consisted of two sets of doors; behind the first of these were a receptionist and a cloakroom where Mitsuoka took off his Japanese-style coat and handed it to an attendant in a bow tie. Then he opened the inner door slightly and peered inside. I left my coat and muffler with the same attendant and caught a quick glance at the interior of the club. Judging from the faces and demeanors of the customers, I could tell it wasn't a shady establishment but rather a high-class club with a respectable clientele. Mitsuoka didn't go inside but instead parted a green curtain next to the cloakroom. A well-cleaned carpet covered a stairway.

"The upstairs is also part of this establishment, but it's rarely used." Mitsuoka went up the stairs, and I followed in a state of uneasiness. On the other side of a heavy wooden door was another counter on which bottles of foreign liquors were lined up. Aside from that, the room looked like the president's office at my company. Next to a large vase with a floral arrangement was a long, plush sofa.

"Make yourself comfortable. This place belongs to me." He fetched a bottle of Scotch and some glasses.

It suddenly occurred to me that after all we had been high school buddies and that I could be candid. "Comfortable? You've got to be kidding! I'm just a regular guy, and I want to get out of here right now. You've become a gangster. We inhabit different worlds."

"Yeah, that's true." Mitsuoka filled my glass with Scotch and flashed his narrow eyes at me. "Actually, we were lying in wait for you today. Tsugawa'll be here soon. The driver just went to call him."

The blood drained from my face. There was something I wasn't sure I should talk to him about, since it was certain that he wouldn't believe it anyway. It was something I had thought I could never talk about no matter what, but Mitsuoka had forced the issue.

"After Tsugawa and I were expelled, what was school life like for you during the six months until you graduated?"

"I followed all the school rules and was careful not to do anything that would attract attention."

"Was that all?"

"Well, I was pretty intense about studying for entrance exams."

"Then, was everything I heard a lie? Every Saturday afternoon you were ordered by Idiot Shorty to go to the judo drill hall where he made you do push-ups after taking off your trousers and underpants."

I felt a violent rush of blood and was unable to look Mitsuoka in the face. All I could think about was who could possibly have told him about an incident I assumed was locked away in the sweat-reeking closet of the Meitoku Hall along with barbells, dumbbells, and cleaning supplies.

"In fact, I was ordered to go to the Meitoku Hall every Saturday. But all that about taking off my trousers and underpants and doing push-ups—that's just someone's fabrication. I was just made to sit in formal position once every week for two hours, just the same as when the three of us did it."

"What? You had to keep doing that? Tsugawa and I were caught red-handed, so we couldn't make excuses for ourselves. But you never brought cigarettes or porn to school. You were careful about those things."

"I felt ashamed that while you and Tsugawa were expelled I was let off the hook and got to study for the entrance exams. I think maybe I saw my being tormented by that jerk every week as a way of making amends for having wronged you guys." As I said it, I convinced myself that it had actually been so.

"That guy's now a regular at a mah-jongg parlor of mine in Tennōji. Except for when he's on duty, he shows up every evening. I've told my young men there to let him win as they see fit."

I finally turned my eyes back toward Mitsuoka, fixing them on his cold, expressionless face. "Have you met with Idiot Shorty?"

Shaking his head, Mitsuoka glared at me and said, "Let's stop calling him Idiot Shorty. Kamisaka will do. For his distinguished service of having led the judo club to the national championship for two consecutive years four years ago, he now gets a high salary just for coaching it." Then he smiled gloatingly. "Let's do him in."

With the glass of Scotch in my hand, I said nervously, "Don't be a fool. And don't get me mixed up in that." I got up to leave.

"I don't mean actually kill him. I'm talking about ruining him socially. This is a tactic Tsugawa thought up, and he wants to do it as long as you agree."

"Why do you need me to agree to it? Can't the two of you just do it if you want to?"

Mitsuoka gulped down the expensive Scotch straight and, stretching out on the long sofa and pillowing his head with his hands, fixed his gaze on me.

"Don't you feel you were shamed, every week baring your dick and ass in front of that sadist and being made to do push-ups?"

"Sadist?"

"When we heard what you'd been put through, I was furious. Tsugawa picked up a whiskey bottle and smashed it. Since it would sort of be like destroying a human being, Tsugawa's of the opinion that we can't go through with it unless all three of us who were humiliated in the drill hall agree."

"You're quite the humanitarian gangster, aren't you? You've probably done things like this many times, haven't you?"

Mitsuoka gave no answer, but keeping his cold, ominous gaze fixed on me, asked, "How d'ya think I heard about what you were forced to do?"

I unwittingly cast my eyes down. After sitting back down on the sofa, I drank some Scotch and lit a cigarette.

"I heard about it from one of my young men who's Kamisaka's mah-jongg partner. In other words, directly from Kamisaka's mouth. He didn't mention your name, but I knew right off who he was talking about. He said, 'It's the greatest when you can torment someone who's powerless to resist. Once I played on the weakness of three smart-assed students, floored them and swept them over my hip until they couldn't stand up, then made them sit on their knees in the drill hall for three hours. The principal was determined to improve the quality of students and get rid of all those who got out of line, and the two that were the real troublemakers were expelled. Every Saturday after classes ended I tormented the other one in the equipment room. I made him take off his trousers and underpants and do push-ups. He was a really nice-looking kid, and I got quite hooked. I would rather have pulled up the skirt of a girl's school uniform, but it was a boys' school.'"

Mitsuoka stood up and, straightening the hem of his kimono, said, "Shouldn't we make Kamisaka's dream come true? And when his dream comes true that will be the time of his downfall."

My hand was shaking so badly out of anger and humiliation that I could no longer hold my glass. Ashes from my cigarette fell on my trousers. From the other side of the door came a woman's voice, "Mr. Tsugawa is here."

Mitsuoka grunted a reply, and a pudgy man with a kinky perm entered. A woman in a kimono also came into the room and, after closing the door and smoothing her hem with a practiced movement, came over to the table and greeted me with a smile. "I'm glad you came," she said. Then she sat next to Mitsuoka. She was of small stature but with beautiful features, a woman who even in a kimono stirred imaginings of the alluring contours of her firm flesh.

"This is the madam of the establishment." Such was Mitsuoka's introduction, but from one glance it was obvious that she was his woman. I looked at Tsugawa. He seemed to have gained fifteen or sixteen pounds since his high school days, and his ill-becoming kinky perm made him look rather vulgar. But the moment I saw his sculpted nose flanked by freckles, I fondly recalled those high school days when he often made everyone laugh with his witty jokes, outrageous though they no doubt were.

"Nagai, I've been holding a grudge against you," he said as he patted me on the shoulder.

"You've been eating too much tripe. What's with this gut of yours?" I poked Tsugawa's stomach and laughed, though I didn't feel like laughing because I had decided to ruin Kamisaka's life. I added, as if groaning, "He would beat my ass with a wooden sword while I was doing pushups. I wanted to go to college and wanted to avoid being expelled no matter what. Right after you two were forced to leave, four others were expelled, and I . . ."

"Great, then it's settled!" Mitsuoka said then whispered something to the woman.

"The poor guy! Another woman like me will be part of the fallout." The woman left betraying an expression of amusement, quite in contrast to what she had said.

I asked for some assurance of my personal safety, emphasizing that I was nothing but a humble office worker. As Mitsuoka was making preparations to toast the decision, he laughed aloud for the first time. "That goes without saying. None of us three will need to do a thing. Some punks will do all the work, and they don't know anything about us. They'll act on their own initiative." It wasn't just that his short hair was combed straight back; there was something about him that could only be called "gravitas" and that made him seem much older than the other two of us.

After we toasted with Scotch and water, three twenty-ish women came in, all with features that men find attractive. They seemed a bit nervous as they glanced around the room. Mitsuoka asked the age and name of the one that looked most innocent.

"Seventeen. I'm Fukuhara Kaori." Having answered, her tongue darted out little-girlishly.

Looking her over in earnest, Mitsuoka said to Tsugawa, "She's in her second year of high school. What do you think?" Tsugawa nodded silently. In a gentle tone of voice, Mitsuoka asked the other two their ages and names and then told them they could go. Realizing that all three were high school students, I stared at them blankly for some time. Now that he mentioned it, there was something juvenile about them, but at the same time they possessed more charm than the female employees at my company, and their attire showed exquisite taste.

"Please sit down," Mitsuoka said to Kaori, pointing to my side and taking a billfold out of his breast pocket. He placed ten ten-thousand yen bills in Kaori's hand. "This is a very dear friend of mine. You lucked out to start your assignment with such a handsome gentleman, huh?" Kaori smiled and sat down next to me without a hint of timidity.

At the same time, Tsugawa stood up and offered me his hand. "I'll leave now. Nagai, stop by my shop anytime." I shook his hand. He gave me his business card and left, looking as if nothing had happened.

Mitsuoka said to Kaori, "The next time you come to this place, you'll have completely forgotten about my friend here." With that, he tapped her on the back with the back of his hand.

I realized that the conversation in the Lincoln between Mitsuoka and his driver had been staged, all arranged beforehand. About fifteen minutes later I left the club Perion. Kaori followed after me. She leaned coquettishly against me and, putting her arm in mine, whispered, "My heart is pounding."

"Look, just say that we fooled around together. I'm going home."

"It's not because of what you and I are going to do that my heart is pounding."

I stopped in my tracks and glanced at Kaori's glossy cheeks.

"I'm okay about wearing a school uniform and acting out being raped, but when I think about what'll come after that, it kind of gets to me."

Ah, so that's what Tsugawa's strategy was. I decided to keep on feigning ignorance and just enjoy the night with the high school girl Mitsuoka's money had treated me to, just as Kamisaka would do a few days later.

"What's this about acting out being raped?"

Kaori studied my uncomprehending expression and cried, "Oh no, I guess I told the wrong person! Don't mention to the boss that I said that, okay?"

"You mean about pretending to be raped?"

"Yeah, I'd really be in for it if you told him."

"I have no idea what it's all about, so there's no way I could talk about it."

Kaori was relieved and again sidled up to me.

"Hmm, rape? I'd like to try it once, but I'm not enough of a bad guy to actually pull it off, unless maybe if we acted it out, with you as my partner."

"Fine. I'll do anything you like. The boss told me in no uncertain terms not to let you get away even if you said you were going home."

Kaori and I hailed a cab. Oddly, Tsugawa's inarticulateness stuck in my mind; he had been so glib in high school. It occurred to me that such a change was not merely the result of maturity.

"I was told not to let you pay for the hotel." Kaori whispered, bringing her lips so close to my ear that they were practically touching.

ON A SATURDAY AFTERNOON about ten days into the New Year, at the persistent invitation of some coworkers I went to play mah-jongg. More than the game, my mind was drawn to the horse races, and I was constantly glancing at the parlor owner, who was glued to the TV and had a tip sheet spread out in front of him.

"We always get hung up on the final round. Let's raise the stakes. Otherwise Nagai's attention will be elsewhere. He's just watching the horses and is too slow at drawing and discarding tiles." One of my coworkers pulled a sour face as he lightly pounded a corner of the mah-jongg table. After the horses for the main race appeared in the lineup, the program was interrupted by a news spot. Declaring that I was only one tile short of going out, I cast an unconcerned glance at the screen, which was showing a mug shot of Kamisaka.

"Hold on a second," I said to my three coworkers as I listened intently to the announcer's voice. The announcer reported that the night before a high school teacher had picked up a female student on her way home and abused her. Based on the accusation of the abused high school student, he was arrested and had pleaded guilty. The announcer said Kamisaka was the coach of XX High School's judo club, which he had led to the national championship for two successive years and which was well known in high school judo circles. The school principal, still familiar though having aged a good deal, appeared on the screen and with a serious demeanor responded to an interviewer's questions.

"Wasn't that your high school, Nagai?"

It was only a short news spot followed by commercials, after which the program went back to the horse races. I didn't answer anyone's questions and just stared at my own tiles. But I gave no thought to such things as being only one tile short. It all came back to me: Kamisaka's voice barking "twenty-one, twenty-two, twenty-three, . . ." the tip of the wooden sword he was holding, the sensation when he forced it with all his might between my exposed buttocks as I lay face down. . . . Why had I gone to see that vile man every Saturday? What did I do there? What did that wooden sword eventually turn into? And the viler he was, did I relax all the more as he praised my good looks?

"Hey, are you already spent?"

Pretending to be afraid of the wooden sword, I would continue doing pushups. Every time my strength gave out, my butt would keep going up and down.

"Thirty-two, thirty-three, thirty-four . . . Hey, do it right! I won't count it if it's just your butt moving."

In order to hide the embarrassing form my penis had assumed, I would take a break, breathing roughly. That vile man would then lightly lift my waist. What had I felt as I waited for that moment? The viler he was, the more I turned into a pure, defenseless woman of incomparable beauty. . . .

Phantom Lights

幻の光

YESTERDAY I TURNED THIRTY-TWO. Three years have passed since I married and moved from Amagasaki in Hyōgo Prefecture to Sosogi on the far coast of the Noto Peninsula, so seven years have gone by since you died and left me.

I'm sitting by an upstairs window basking in the warm spring sunshine and looking out at the calm sea and at my husband's car as he leaves for work. Watching the vehicle, now tiny as it recedes along the tortuously winding road that hugs the shoreline, I feel my body constricting as if turning into a tight bud.

I'm sure you know how on a smooth green sea—the kind you seldom see here—there will be one area that's a glistening mass. It looks like great schools of fish surging up from beneath the sea, their dorsal fins showing among the waves, but it's really only a lot of ripples. Though not clear to the eye what it is, there are times when light dances like that on the surface of the sea and only part of the wavelets are illuminated. My father-in-law told me this plays a trick on your mind if you're looking from a distance. I don't understand exactly what kind of trick, but I have caught myself several times staring absently at those clusters of light on the ripples. What he may have been trying to say is that to the weary eyes of the down-and-out fishermen in these parts—people who've never had the fortune of a good catch—the ripples are disquieting, like flashes of a dream. But when I heard him talk about it, it appeared to mean something else. Or so it seemed, but I had no idea what that meaning might have been.

Sosogi is a poor town where the sea roars all year long. In winter, the wind from the Sea of Japan is so strong that it sweeps away any snow that might fall. The fact that the sea is warmer than the snow or the air also has something to do with it, but they say that it is mostly because the wind blows snow away before it can accumulate. Even in years with heavy snowfalls, only scattered patches form along the seashore. Together with the freezing wind there is only the frenzied sound of waves and spray arising like moist, pitch-black dust.

The west side of town, where the Machino River empties into Sosogi Harbor, is visible over the roof of the house next door. That's the only place along the shore around here that has anything like a sandy beach. Everywhere else, in a jagged line stretching from the light house on Saruyama in the west to the beacon on the eastern end, it is rocky and not suited for swimming even where it's shallow. Fishing harbors here and there exist in name only now; almost no boats go out. Even here in Sosogi Harbor, two or three small fishing craft, the names on their hulls almost completely faded away, lie neglected on the beach. People who are unaccustomed to the sound of the waves—for example the tourists who go out of their way to come and hear it—end up defeated by it and are annoyed when it awakens them in the middle of the night. Strange, but today both the wind and the waves have come to a standstill. Everything is bathed in a warm glow, and I can't hear anything aside from an occasional passing automobile or what seems to be the sound of someone in the neighborhood hanging laundry out to dry.

Days like this are rare, so I ought to be airing out the quilts and cushions and seeing to a lot of other chores. But such days always make me feel drained, and I can't muster the will to do anything. The sight of you, your shoulders hunched, walking away along the tracks just after the rain—no matter how I try to clear it from my mind it always emerges from some recess of my consciousness. Two years have passed since I brought our son Yūichi here and married into Sekiguchi Tamio's family. In spite of all my efforts, I have been unable to stop the monologue that has run unconsciously in my mind since the day you died.

An example: Yūichi sees you get off the bus from Wajima even though you are supposed to be dead and comes running breathlessly to tell me about it. At that moment, a burning instantly wells up in my breast making my entire body shake, and I run to the bus stop on trembling legs.

How many times have I imagined such idiotic, dream-like scenes and then looked about to make sure that no one has noticed the slight movement of my lips?

In these parts, people in their prime all leave for the cities. It's impossible to make a living here from fishing alone, and where rice is grown in small paddies, it doesn't provide a year's subsistence. A few lucky ones can work for the local government or in the post office, but there is hardly any other place around here for anyone else to find employment. After completing junior high or high school, both boys and girls get jobs far away. And it isn't only the young people; even men in their forties or fifties leave their families to go to Tokyo or Osaka to work. We're among the fortunate ones. Tamio is employed as a chef at a large tourist inn in Wajima, and during the spring and summer travel season we convert one downstairs and two upstairs rooms of our house into bed-and-breakfast lodgings, which I manage. We're always short of cash, but somehow we make ends meet so that we can all stay together. Tamio is a quiet man with a gentle nature. Tomoko, the daughter from his previous marriage, has taken to me. But even so I have secretly gone on talking to you—you who willfully abandoned your wife and infant to go off and die.

A long time ago, when both of us were about twenty, you were looking at the freckles scattered beneath my eyes and, fixing your peculiar gaze on me as if your mind were elsewhere, said, "Yumi, I'll bet you're still hiding lots more freckles."

We had been close friends since childhood, but that was the first time you said something that somehow made me uneasy. I felt a wrenching in the pit of my stomach, but I just pretended to be embarrassed and smiled back. At the time, I thought I understood what you meant by that comment, but now whenever I think of you and your senseless suicide I realize that you weren't talking about my body. Your remark was annoying, and as we pressed our fingers together I couldn't help thinking that even before we were married, you had hit onto that part of my feminine psyche that is sensitive to such things. The more I think about the significance of those freckles the more complicated it all becomes, and I understand less and less the reasons for your suicide.

Sometimes I think I must be a perverse sort of woman for talking like this to my deceased former husband even while living peacefully with my new spouse. But it's a habit now, and at some point I began talking not so much to you—and not really to my own heart either—but to something more indescribable, intimate, and dear, and I become totally absorbed as if in a trance. I have no idea exactly what that "intimate and dear" thing is. Why were you trudging along the tracks of the Hanshin Line that night, knowing full well that you would be run over?

ABOUT TEN DAYS BEFORE you died, your bicycle was stolen. It would have taken two bus transfers to get to the screw factory where you worked, and it was too far to walk. You had said it would be a waste to go by bus, so we tightened our belts to buy that bicycle. I wonder why we had so many expenses then, one after another. It was three months after Yūichi was born, so there was the cost of the delivery. All kinds of petty expenses piled up, and our savings had about vanished. What's more, the screw factory subcontracted with other subcontractors, and the pay was pathetically low.

"Damn! Since I had mine stolen, I'll go steal one myself!"

You stormed out of the apartment the next day, a Sunday, and that evening came riding home on a bicycle you really had stolen.

"As long as I was going to steal one, I thought I'd get a rich guy's bike, and I walked clear to Kōshien to find one."

I didn't feel that it was such a crime either, and even said with a laugh, "Now that you've got a taste of stealing, don't turn into a real thief." You sprawled out next to me as I was nursing Yūichi and stared at the ceiling for a long time. You seemed old for your twenty-five years, and your reddish lips, a distinguishing feature of yours since childhood, appeared too red next to your hollow cheeks. I felt vaguely apprehensive, and said, "You'd better paint it a different color so it can't be identified. If its owner happened to see it, it'd be pretty serious."

The tepid rays of the setting winter sun were filtering through the window of our cramped kitchen. Whatever else we did, we would have to buy an air conditioner for Yūichi next summer. Since it was just a modest, six-mat room, a small one would do. Such listless thoughts passed through my mind as I listened to the footsteps of someone going up and down the stairs of the apartment building.

"A mechanic who's a customer of ours hired a sumo wrestler."

"Huh? A sumo wrestler?"

"He didn't show much promise as a wrestler and had retired from the ring when he was hired as an assistant truck driver for this mechanic. He's probably already past thirty and still has his hair done up in a topknot, but he's completely under the thumb of the driver, who's about eighteen or nineteen. I couldn't stand the sight of that topknot."

"Hmm . . . Why's that?"

"I'm not really sure. Why doesn't he just cut the thing off?"

"Did you really walk to Kōshien?"

You rolled over in bed so that you were lying face down on the tatami and said, laughing as you looked aside at Yūichi, "Somehow looking at that topknot makes me depressed."

"Oh, there goes that squint of yours again."

Sometimes, after you stared sideways at something, your left eye would stay in that position, making you temporarily cross-eyed. This time, your left eye was straining to the side so much that it gave me a start, and I blurted that out without thinking.

You hurriedly rubbed your eye, your back turned to me as if to indicate your bad mood. For a long time you kept rubbing your left eye with the back of your hand.

"I only finished junior high, so I'm not good for much. I'll never have much money."

You must have been depressed after stealing a bicycle in a quiet residential neighborhood in Kōshien and riding it to this back alley in Amagasaki.

"Maybe, but compared to when I was a kid, I'm a lot happier since I married you."

When I said that, you rolled over to face me. "Really?" Your bloodshot left eye was turned outward even more, and you looked like a completely different person. It usually went right back to normal, but that day for some reason, no matter how much you rubbed it, it wouldn't correct itself.

Yūichi had fallen asleep. After moving him to the baby bed, I straddled you and massaged your left eye, pressing down with the palm of my hand.

"It'll straighten out soon enough. It hurts if you massage it too much. Sometimes the muscle that moves the eyeball gets a cramp."

"It must hurt, then. Doesn't it hurt behind your eyes?"

"It feels tight and heavy, but there's no pain. It's best just to leave it alone."

Just as you said, within thirty minutes it had corrected itself, but that face you made—one that looked liked someone else's—was etched permanently in my mind. Why didn't it occur to me then that those strange, occasional spasms in your eye were actually an expression of your inner self? Why wasn't I able to see in that crossed left eye of yours a sign that ten days later you would commit suicide?

That day, it had been raining since morning. The rain stopped about seven o'clock, and, except for Yūichi's diapers, I hung out all of the laundry that had been drying in our room. On the street below our window, three "love hotels" stood next to each other, the red and blue of their neon signs mixing to bathe everything in a murky purple. Evenings after rain, the effect was even more pronounced, dyeing the interior of our apartment a depressing hue.

It was past eleven, but you still hadn't come home. That wasn't like you, and it made me feel somehow uneasy. Yūichi was fussing, so I lay down with him in my bed and ended up falling asleep with the lights on. I was startled awake by a knock on the door, and glanced at the clock: 3:00 a.m. Thinking you had come home, I opened the door to see the caretaker of the apartment building together with a policeman. The caretaker asked, "Your husband?"

"He hasn't come home yet." The instant I answered, a chill ran down my spine. I sensed that something had happened to you, and I doubt that I'll ever again experience such a horrible presentiment.

The policeman said in a low voice, "There's a man who's been hit by a train. Would you be willing to identify him?"

"What? Is it my husband?" Even as I spoke, a chilling certainty that it was in fact you left me unable to say more.

"The corpse is in bad shape. We couldn't have you tell by looking at the face, but maybe you could identify it by the clothing, shoes, or some small personal effects."

I left Yūichi with the caretaker and his wife and got into the patrol car parked in front of the entrance. The policeman explained as he drove: Stuck to a tattered piece from the trousers was a scrap of an envelope on which was printed "Okajima Screw Factory."

"Of the three employees of the Okajima Screw Factory, only your husband hadn't yet returned home. We walked back and forth along the railway for three hours before we found that scrap of paper."

The only remaining articles were a shoe and a key to the apartment, and both were without question yours. The corpse was so mangled and broken that it couldn't be put together, and they wouldn't show it to me. A toe was found the next morning, and from its print the corpse was positively identified as yours.

It happened between Kuise and Daimotsu. According to the engineer, you were walking right between the tracks with your back to the train. It was just after a gentle curve in the line, and by the time you appeared in the headlights, it was too late. You didn't turn around either at the sound of the horn or the horrible screeching of the brakes but just kept walking straight ahead until the moment you were hit. He said that about six standing passengers were knocked down and injured by the sudden stop.

No one considered it anything but a suicide, and even the newspaper reported it as such in small print. But I remained unconvinced. I couldn't think of any possible reason why you would kill yourself. The police, too, investigated from various angles but could find no motive. No evidence of drugs or alcohol was found on the corpse. You were in good health and didn't drink; you didn't gamble; you had no relations with other women; and you didn't have the sort of debts that would drive you to your death. On the contrary, your first child was three months old, a time when men are in high spirits. Even the police officers were perplexed; they couldn't find a single motive for your death.

Every time I recall those days following your death, it seems a wonder that I didn't lose my mind. Sometimes I felt at a loss, other times as if people had conspired to deceive me. Deep within my dazed heart was another heart that could neither cry nor scream, that just kept sinking into the darkest depths of the earth. The caretaker and his wife began keeping a constant watch on me. Perhaps they were worried because I ignored Yūichi's crying and just stared vacantly at the tatami. "Maybe they think I'm going to follow my husband in death by turning on the gas or something," I thought, as if it had nothing to do with myself. I wasn't considering suicide with Yūichi, but neither was I giving thought to how we were going to go on living. An image of you from behind, trudging along the tracks after the rain, kept flashing through the recesses of my mind. Desperate to know what you were thinking, my thoughts kept following after the familiar figure of your grey blazer over a pale blue shirt, your back slightly hunched as you walked, alone and mute, along the tracks in the dead of night.

I wonder how many days passed like that. Eventually I began to imagine that you would sometimes stop your silent procession and turn and face me, your hair blowing in the cold wind. The face that looked back at me in the dim light was the same cross-eyed one I had seen that night you stole the bicycle. Whenever I saw that face, an immense sadness would overcome me, and I would stare motionlessly as you receded into the distance.

"Twenty-five . . . That's young for a widow," both Mom and my brother, Kenji, would say with a sigh every time they dropped by. Two months passed without my doing much of anything. From the ads in the newspaper, I learned that the love hotel right in front of the apartment was looking for a woman to clean and staff the desk, so I went for an interview. I arranged for my mother, who had been living with my brother, to move into my apartment and take care of Yūichi. That sort of work went against my inclinations, but because of the location I could sometimes come home when I had nothing to do. Also, I had heard that it could provide a decent income and that once in a while a customer might tip me.

We first got to know each other when we were in sixth grade, which would have been in 1957, a year full of ominous happenings in my family.

At that time, we were living in a large wooden apartment building on the Hanshin Highway in Amagasaki. The building had a rather strange configuration: a large apartment, looking like an architectural afterthought, had been built above what was originally two tenement houses on either side of a path, making one building out of the two with a tunnel running right through the middle linking the highway and the back alley. Sunlight never reached the inside of the tunnel, where a naked light bulb was on constantly. The soil was always damp, and there was a disagreeable odor. Above the tunnel was a hallway for the second floor, and the sound of footsteps echoed loudly. People in the neighborhood never referred to the building by its proper name of Matsuda Apartments but called it the "tunnel tenement."

My family lived on the first floor near the middle of the tunnel, where several apartments were concentrated. Next to us on the south was a communal lavatory. All year the strong odor of deodorizer seeped through the earthen walls. If we dashed out to the front street on a sunny day, our eyes would be so dazzled by the brightness that we would momentarily stop in our tracks.

In the apartment to the north of ours lived a family that operated a mobile noodle stall. During the rainy season one year when the downpour hadn't let up for several days on end, we wondered aloud, "They must be having a tough time of it next door, since they can't do any business." One day, when no voices could be heard through the thin walls, Dad went to check on the situation and found that the couple had hanged themselves after strangling their two daughters with a cord.

That night, Dad was led away by the police. According to the suicide note, whatever money they had left was to be used for taking care of the remains and the money could be found in an envelope on the desk. Yet no money could be found anywhere. Since Dad was the first one on the scene after the suicide, suspicion fell on him. He would never even think of doing such a thing. He didn't have a strong constitution and lacked assertiveness but was called in time and time again. The harshness of the investigations seemed to take their toll; he was bedridden for a long time after that.

We were a family of five then: Mom and Dad, myself, my brother Kenji (three years younger), and eighty-three-year-old Grandma. Grandma was Dad's mother. She got around alright but was hard of hearing and senile. She was from Sukumo in Shikoku, and after Grandpa died, Dad took her in to live with us. But for someone who had spent her life in a spacious country area, a cramped and dank dwelling in Amagasaki was more than she could bear.

About a year before the suicide next door, Grandma tried running away. After that she was watched by the police, coming under surveillance when she went about asking passers-by how to get to Sukumo in Shikoku. She would walk along streetcar tracks or cross the street nonchalantly even when the light was red, oblivious to the danger.

"Even if you made it back to Shikoku, there's no home there to return to. You'd need a boat to cross the sea, so it doesn't matter how determined you are to walk. You couldn't make it back." Our attempts to convince her were useless; she was senile, and it didn't get through to her.

It was the hottest part of summer. Countless trucks were rushing past on the highway, shaking the ground, their black exhaust filling the tunnel through the apartment building. I dashed out to the front, holding my breath. I was certain Grandma had been sleeping in the three-mat room just a while ago, but she was now walking down the highway in the direction of Kōbe. I raced down the sultry, dusty road, ran in front of Grandma and stopped to block her way. Then I put my mouth to her ear and yelled in a loud voice, "If you're out wandering again, Dad'll be furious at you. Now, go back home. It's hot out, so go back home."

Grandma's wrinkled face broke into a smile, and she said in a barely audible voice, "I want to die in Sukumo. I'm going back to Shikoku."

It was a tone of voice I had never heard from her, one that wouldn't take no for an answer. She shoved me aside and again started walking.

For a while I stood motionless, staring at Grandma's retreating figure. I suddenly came to my senses, raced home and reported the situation to Dad, who had been in bed since the incident with the police. He got up in a start and was about to go chase after her but then stopped.

"Oh, leave her alone! Someone will bring her back this time too. We can't very well tie her to a post."

Dad looked completely exhausted and collapsed in a corner of the dim room. I went looking for Mom. Since Dad was in that condition, Mom had started working for a building contractor in the neighborhood. Along with the men, she helped cart blocks and plywood to a building site in front of Amagasaki Station on the Hanshin Line. With the towel over her straw hat tied under her chin, Mom was pushing the cart in the blazing heat of the construction site.

I came running up out of breath. As I was about to call out to her, one of the men kicked her in the rear. "I don't give a damn if you're a woman. If I catch you goldbricking, you won't get paid."

I forgot about Grandma and darted away from there as fast as I could. I kept running aimlessly through the long shopping arcade, its floor checkered by light streaming through broken roof panels. When I stopped, out of breath and soaked with perspiration, a chill swept across my legs from my knees down. From the opening and closing glass doors of a large pachinko parlor, a cold draft from the air conditioner was creeping along the ground. I unbuttoned my blouse and wiped the perspiration with the hem of my skirt. Then I staggered into the pachinko parlor. A buxom woman with the face of an ogre was chewing gum as she played. I ambled back and forth for a while among the machines, and the perspiration began to feel like ice water. But my abdomen was burning, and I felt awful.

The reason I remember that day so clearly is that it was right there in the pachinko parlor that I had my first period. They had told us in our school's health class how to take care of it, but I panicked anyway and dashed into the restroom. I was in there for a long time, at a loss for what to do. Eventually, an employee came and knocked on the door several times, probably thinking it strange that the door remained locked. I folded up a wad of toilet paper and applied it to the bleeding, pulled my bloody panties up, and walked out as if nothing had happened. With my hands pressed over the front and back of my skirt, I walked home ever so slowly. Even when the perspiration rolled off my bobbed bangs and into my eyes, I refused to move my hands from my skirt.

When I got home, I went into the inner three-mat room, closed the tattered sliding door, and sat on the floor motionlessly, my legs tucked under me.

"Yumiko, I'm getting kind of worried after all. Won't you go look for Grandma?" Dad asked as he pushed the door open and peered inside. He noticed that I was not my usual self and kept asking what was wrong.

"My stomach hurts," I answered. An unbearable sadness came over me. It wasn't that I was afraid of this first sign of adulthood; at that moment, for the first time in my life I despised poverty. Grandma's slight figure as she vanished down the highway under the blazing sun, the sight of Mom being kicked in the rear by that laborer, the dank room where a light bulb has to burn all day—all of these images sprang to mind. I shut the sliding door with a bang and continued to press my skirt over my panties, now crusted with dried blood. The reason I'm overcome even now by an inexplicable, chilly sadness when I have my period is probably that icy air in the pachinko parlor where I had my first one.

Until late that night we assumed that we would eventually hear from some police station somewhere. Dad reluctantly got up and went to the neighborhood police box, but there had been no report of such an elderly person in custody. "She doesn't have a penny on her and wouldn't have had the slightest idea which train to get on anyway, so it's unlikely that she's been able to get very far. Let's just wait until tomorrow. It's summer, so it's not as if she'll freeze to death on the road." The policeman made these suggestions nonchalantly, with a look of exasperation on his face. But Grandma disappeared as if spirited away, and we never saw her again.

We contacted relatives and had them arrange with police in various places to begin searches, but a week passed, then two weeks, and we still knew nothing of Grandma's whereabouts. Could it be that she had a secret cache of money and kept asking directions until she boarded a boat at Kobe and miraculously made it back to her destination of Sukumo? Mom and Dad both thought of that and inquired through express letters to friends and acquaintances in Shikoku. To make sure, the police also arranged for searches by police stations throughout Shikoku, but they did not find Grandma.

In mid-December, after six months had passed, the familiar policeman dropped by our house and said, "Either she's been taken in by some benevolent person who looks after unidenti-fied lost elderly people, or she's fallen into a river or the sea and her body didn't come to the surface. I can't think of any other possibilities."

By that time, both Mom and Dad were hoping that Grand-ma would not be found. It's not something that they would have said aloud, but I'm sure they were hoping that she had died somewhere.

Then the policeman, who until then had spoken in a calm tone of voice, suddenly went on with a searching look in his eyes. "Actually, a lot of rumors have been circulating in the neighborhood. People are saying that now that things aren't chaotic the way they were when the war ended, it doesn't make sense that a helpless old person should be lost."

"Yeah, well, that's occurred to us too, since she's our own flesh and blood."

"I'd like to search your apartment. Do you mind?"

"Our apartment?"

"I want to take up the mats and dig underneath the floor-boards."

"What! Are you saying that we killed Grandma and buried her under the floorboards?"

Shocked, Dad looked at Mom, who was blue in the face as she glared back at the policeman. Suspicion had fallen on Dad because the matter of the money purportedly left by the noo-dle shop owners who committed suicide had not been com-pletely cleared up. Mild-mannered Dad, quaking by then, said to the policeman in a high voice as if issuing a challenge, "Oh, please, go right ahead and search the whole house or anywhere you like! If you find Grandma, it will surely be our doing. And maybe you'll even find the money that the people next door left behind. When they're driven to desperation by poverty, people will kill their own parents if they become a burden and pocket other people's money, won't they? Why wait for tomor-row? Why not dig up the floor now?"

"Hm? Okay, then, we'll do that." With that, the policeman left. About three hours later, a patrol car and a pickup truck stopped in the back alley, and five or six policemen dressed in grey overalls came into the house with shovels. With the landlord looking on, they moved chests of drawers and cupboards outside, took up the tatami, and began digging. Exchanging furtive whispers, the residents of the tenement house gathered.

I was trembling as I clung to Mom. Even though I had watched with my own eyes as Grandma disappeared heading west on the Hanshin Highway, I was plagued by an apprehension that her corpse might actually be exhumed from the damp black soil beneath the floor.

Nothing turned up. It was evening before the policeman left with a disagreeable look on his face after hurriedly putting things back in place. Even after shoveling the earth back into place, re-laying the tatami, and putting the shabby chests of drawers and cupboards back where they were, the odor of the soil seemed to keep seeping out.

Mom lay down in a corner of the room. I rested my head in her lap as I sprawled out next to her. "Yumiko, you shouldn't be wearing baby skirts like this. You're a young lady now, and it's embarrassing to have your panties showing."

"Yeah, but since that time, it hasn't happened again."

As Mom played with my hair, making it into braids, she said with a laugh, "It's like that at first. Some girls go a year or two between periods." The ridge of her nose and the backs of her hands were tanned, and she seemed to have aged a lot in the last year.

"Your father will be working again next year, and I'll be quitting the building contractor and working at Otafuku, the *okonomiyaki* shop Otafuku in front of the station. The woman who had been working there quit, and I'm taking her place."

"Huh? Otafuku?"

"You have a face just like Otafuku."

"Mom, am I pretty? Or plain?"

"You'll get pretty from now on."

"So, that means I'm plain now."

The tatami and the furniture were all supposed to have been returned to where they had been, but somehow it felt as if we were lying in a rearranged room and were not yet used to it. Looking at the slightly flickering fluorescent light that was nearing the end of its life, I felt a sense of relief that I had never before experienced. "Relief" definitely describes the feeling I had then. Ah, Grandma had no doubt died somewhere, Dad would be working, Mom wouldn't have to put up with the building contractor anymore, and I had had my first period. All those thoughts passed through my mind in an instant, and for that brief moment I basked in a feeling of relief.

The next day I saw you for the first time. In the apartment at the far end of the building, facing the back alley, lived a middle-aged widower named Nakaoka. You were the son of the gentle-mannered woman who moved in as his second wife.

When I got home from school, you were pitching a ball against the high brick fence by the side of the tunnel tenement, your blue baseball cap askew on your head. I passed by, stealing sidelong glances at the unfamiliar boy playing by himself, but somehow I couldn't get him out of my mind. There wasn't anything particularly remarkable about him, so why was I so preoccupied with him? Until dusk, I stole several glances from a distance as you tossed the ball against the brick fence.

Three years later—about the same time your mother passed away—Grandma, whose corpse was never found, was legally declared dead and her name was removed from the family register. To this day, twenty years later, her remains have not turned up. If she were still alive, she'd be over a hundred by now, and that couldn't very well be the case. The more I think about it, the more I'm convinced that no one has died a more mysterious death. It was a strange disappearance, and then you appeared before me as if to replace Grandma who had left this world. It somehow seems eerie.

ON THE REMOTE COAST of the Noto Peninsula, the weather is capricious. One minute it will be clear and pleasant, and suddenly the clouds and waves will start swelling, making it seem as if night has fallen all around. It was on such a day three years ago that I came here for the first time with four-year old Yūichi. After transferring to the Nanao Line at Kanazawa, I watched from the train as the entire peninsula went from spring back to winter, becoming dark and cold as the skies cleared and then clouded up again.

I had left Amagasaki at seven o'clock that morning. After saying goodbye to the landlord couple, who had brought up this prospect of remarriage and who had helped me in so many ways, I walked with my mother to Amagasaki Station on the Hanshin Line. In the park in front of the station, the cherry blossoms had nearly all scattered, the petals swept up in clouds by the strong wind.

Mom, who hadn't shed a tear when you died, stood next to me crying as I purchased the tickets. Office workers hurrying by in the early morning rush turned to look at us.

"Yumiko, if you don't like it there, come back anytime. You can live with me."

"OK, if I don't like it, I won't put up with it. I'll come back."

"What kind of talk is that? Once a woman marries, she's part of her husband's family and has to grin and bear it. If you think that way, you shouldn't consider remarrying in the first place," Mom said, contradicting herself as she hugged Yūichi.

My younger brother, Kenji, an automobile salesman who was still single, backed up Mom's promise, saying, "Don't worry. I could take care of one or two mothers." I felt relieved to hear that. After talking Mom out of seeing me as far as Osaka Station, I stopped again and again to look back as I climbed the steps to the platform.

Jostled by the crowd, I gazed for a while over the streets of Amagasaki, where I had been born and raised. It hit home to me then why it was that I wanted to go off as a bride to a desolate fishing village on the northernmost tip of the Noto Peninsula. It wasn't because I was so taken by the thirty-five-year-old Sekiguchi Tamio, who had brought his eight-year old daughter all the way from Noto to Amagasaki to meet me. It wasn't because I had grown sick of Amagasaki, surrounded by pollution, the neon of saunas and cabarets, and shabby apartment buildings. Nor was it because I hated working in the love hotel, spreading sheets in which raw odors lingered. I wanted to run away from all of the sights, sounds, and smells associated with you. Along with that realization, for some reason that last image of Grandma as she walked west under the blazing sun on the Hanshin Highway came to life vividly in my mind. Suddenly I could hardly keep from running back to Mom, who was no doubt still standing by the ticket collector's gate. If I hadn't met Mrs. Kan with her children then, I'm sure I'd have run down the stairs from the platform with Yūichi in my arms.

Mrs. Kan was a Korean who cut her hair in a masculine style, wore men's work clothes, drove a pickup truck by herself, and ran a business collecting scrap. She was only thirty-eight but looked about ten years older with her prominent red cheekbones. She had a seven year-old boy and a five year-old girl by the hand on either side and an eight-month-old infant strapped to her back. She was waiting for a train, wearing her usual work clothes. She was usually surly, but that day as soon as she saw my face she approached and asked, "Where are you headed this early in the morning?"

Since I knew only the usual masculine Mrs. Kan who always had a cigarette in her mouth and drove a truck, I was caught off guard by the unexpectedly gentle, feminine tone of voice. I answered honestly, "I'm headed for Noto."

"Noto? Where's that?"

"Ishikawa Prefecture, the upper part."

"What are you going to a place like that for?"

The express bound for Umeda came in. Casting a sidelong glance at me as I stood at a loss whether or not to run back down to the ticket gate, Mrs. Kan let go of the boy's hand, casually took Yūichi into her arms, and shouted, "Jump in and get a seat for this lady!" As soon as the door opened, the boy slipped in around the legs of passengers getting off and, throwing himself into some empty seats, cried out, "I got some, Mom, I got some!"

Before I could say anything, Mrs. Kan boarded the train with Yūichi. I had no choice but to get on myself.

"Hmm, so you're going to remarry?"

At Mrs. Kan's loud voice, the nearby passengers all turned and looked at me. I was embarrassed and tried to change the subject by asking, "Well, where are *you* headed so early in the morning?"

"To the zoo in Tennōji. It's Saturday, and since I'm free this morning I thought I'd take the kids."

"It must be hard taking three kids."

"Tell me about it! But they've been pestering me to take them."

As I was rocked by the train, I thought that after I got to Umeda, I would turn around and go back to Amagasaki. But as soon as we got to Umeda, Mrs. Kan said she would see me to Osaka Station.

"We left too early anyway, so we've got time on our hands. Now, let's not stand on ceremony. We'll never see each other again, after all." Hurrying my pace to catch up to Mrs. Kan, who had started off ahead with vigorous strides, I thought to myself that I would go as far as Sosogi and that if I didn't feel right about the whole thing I could turn around and come back, just as Mom had said.

Mrs. Kan went to the platform and waited with us for the arrival of the train, the Thunderbolt 2. It seemed as if she wanted to say something. She kept opening her mouth only to close it and remain silent. Looking at her and the two unkempt children, for some reason tears welled in my eyes. I thought it strange that Mrs. Kan, with whom I'd never once had a heart-to-heart talk, should see me to the platform like this.

"A woman's best years are just starting for you. Good luck!" she said with a determined look on her face. "Once you get him firmly between your legs, a man is reduced to putty. The trick is to win over his kids. I'm not joking. That's really how you go about it."

The arrival of the train was announced. I nodded in acknowledgment of what she had said and hurried off to catch Yūichi, who was running around on the platform.

As the train moved off, Mrs. Kan roughly strapped the baby to her back and, taking the two other children by the hand, stood motionlessly on the platform, her gold tooth shining as she smiled. I had known Mrs. Kan for ten years, but this was the first time I saw her smile.

What was it that Mrs. Kan put into my mind, which was already a stew of anxiety, uncertainty, and regret jostled by the motion of the train? Why did she see me off at the platform, though we had never once exchanged an intimate word? Sometimes I dream of going off on a vacation somewhere with Mrs. Kan and her children. Though she was tight-fisted about everything else, in my dreams her gold tooth, on which she had spent money unsparingly, shone with a mysterious elegance.

At Kanazawa we transferred to the Nanao Line, on which the train stops at every station, so it took three-and-a-half hours to get to Wajima. Yūichi, who had been excited about his first long trip, was thoroughly bored by the time we got to Kanazawa, and on the Nanao Line he went racing about, getting knocked over again and again by the violent jerking of the ancient car. By the time we reached Nanao he had fallen asleep, and I was able to relax and turn my attention to the scenery outside. On the left, the low mountains were surrounded by narrow paddies and fields, while on the right the sea was visible in the distance. As the train proceeded to the tip of the peninsula, the sky grew gradually darker. Whenever we stopped at one of the larger stations, crowds of homeward-bound junior high and high school students would board, their numbers gradually decreasing with each stop until they had all gotten off again. Then a new crowd would board. Not unlike their urban counterparts, they would cast impertinent glances at me and my child.

All the way to Wajima I talked to you, a dead man, as I looked out the window. I don't even remember what I said, but without realizing it I had already gotten into the habit of talking to you whenever I was alone. And the image I always had of you when I talked to you was your retreating figure as you walked down the tracks. Merely imagining that figure sent a chill through my heart, but whenever I talked to it, I got the distinct feeling that a different heart of mine was falling into a strange, intoxicating sort of ecstasy.

How happy I was to hear from your own lips the words "I love you." I've never known greater happiness in all my life.

Neither of us had gone further than junior high school. I wanted to see my younger brother Kenji at least graduate from high school, so I wasn't particularly upset when Mom told me to give up pursuing an education. Dad was bedridden with a protracted illness, and I knew very well that he wouldn't be able to send two children to high school. But you stubbornly turned down the chance to continue your schooling and instead began working as an apprentice at a steel plant, I suppose because your mother passed away when you were in the ninth grade and you didn't want to be a burden to your stepfather. You were studious and good-looking, so I had a lot of rivals for your affection. When most of those rivals went on to high school, it felt as if just the two of us had been left alone in a small room somewhere, and I was on a high. From then until adulthood we went through various trials, but my feelings for you never faded.

We married, and three months after the birth of our child I lost you through a senseless suicide. Since then I've lived on as an empty shell. My dazed mind kept wondering why you killed yourself, what possible reason you could have had. And then I grew so weary of those thoughts that I no longer cared and gave in to the landlord couple's suggestion of remarriage.

It began to rain shortly before we arrived in Wajima. The alarms sounding at each railroad crossing would grow louder and then recede behind us. The houses along the railway gradually became more countrified, what one would expect to find in poor villages.

Misty rain was falling horizontally, driven by a strong wind. The interior of the heated train was actually rather hot, so when we got off at Wajima I was surprised that it was cold enough to make me shiver. It was April, but as chilly as winter. Holding Yūichi, who was still drowsy, I passed through the ticket gate with heavy steps, thinking to myself, "Ah, I've really come to a fine place!" A crowd of people appearing to be tourists were thronging around the ticket gate, and I wasn't able to see Tamio, who was supposed to come meet me. I thought that I should just go back after all. Something was wrong with me. I must have been out of my mind. Why else would I have decided to come to a remote place like the tip of the Noto Peninsula? Such thoughts passed through my tense and nervous mind.

About five minutes later, Tamio and his daughter Tomoko came rushing into the station. He apologized saying there was a group tour from western Japan and that stocking up on things for their meals had taken a lot of time. When her father poked her in the back, eight-year old Tomoko bowed and delivered the line she had no doubt rehearsed, "Thank you for coming."

I made a hasty response, and then we got into Tamio's small car. Leaving the shop-lined streets of Wajima, we continued down a narrow winding road along the sea for nearly half an hour. The dark clouds gradually broke, and an azure sky peeked out. A mass of clouds swirled above the misty rain, and it was impossible to tell whether the weather was about to change for the worse or was clearing up. Through the rain-drop-specked window of the car, I gazed out over the vast, rolling Sea of Japan. We passed through a few small villages and, again coming out onto the road along the shore, I laid eyes on the sea by Sosogi for the first time. I hardly know how to describe its color, completely covered as it was then by the misty rain. It was a dark, undulating sea such as I had never seen before, with the waves blown high in an eerie whiteness.

The Sekiguchis lived in a two-storey house facing the sea. It was old, the only new thing being its retiled roof. Tamio was the oldest son. After completing junior high school, he had gone off to work in a restaurant on the reclaimed land in the Sonezaki area of Osaka, boarding with the proprietor for ten years until he was licensed as a chef. He had planned to remain in Osaka but couldn't neglect his aging parents. It so happened that the tourist inn at Wajima was looking for a chef, and that was the occasion of his return to Sosogi. He married a local woman, who died of illness three years later. The Sekiguchi family also included his sixty-eight-year-old father, who had lost his wife five years before, and three siblings.

Tamio's brothers and sisters lived in Osaka and Nagoya, and I didn't have to deal with a mother-in-law or other in-laws. Once Tamio had seen me to his home, he left again. On Saturdays, the banquets of tour groups would run late. He apologized that it had to be on a day like today, but the proprietor of the inn had been particularly earnest in his request. Tamio left, promising to return as early as possible. I felt somehow relieved and sat down in the ten-mat room downstairs for want of anything else to do. Listening intently, I thought, "Ah, so *that's* the roar of the sea."

My father-in-law suggested, barely audibly, that I just relax today and wait until tomorrow to make my greetings to relatives and neighbors. He wore a padded jacket over his shirt, and the black *tabi* socks on his feet were full of holes. I asked him where I could find the sewing kit, but since there had not been any women in the household for more than two years, he seemed to have no idea. He had suffered a slight stroke four or five years earlier, and since then he had had trouble moving his mouth and right hand. I sat down with him, and his salt-and-pepper close-cropped hair and gentle, wrinkled face eased the anxiety and tenseness that had been gripping me. I was surprised to see that Yūichi, who was usually shy around strangers, responded to the old man's coaxing and went and sat on his knee without hesitation.

Tomoko, dressed in a red sweater and trousers, sat by herself in the spacious, wooden-floored room facing the kitchen. Pretending to be engaged in play, she studied my appearance. Suddenly Mrs. Kan's words came to mind. I went over to Tomoko and said, "Starting today, I'm your mother." She looked up at me and smiled. In that instant I sensed that she was still very much a little girl, and I was able to loosen the knots of uncertainty that had been tightening within me. She had been looking forward to my coming. At that thought my spirits lifted, and everything—the musty atmosphere of the house, the roar of the nearby sea, the chilliness of the room with the darkly shining floorboards, and even the television with its fuzzy reception—felt as familiar as if I had been there for years.

That night, in the eight-mat room upstairs facing the sea, the four of us—Tamio, the children, and I—spread out our quilts next to each other. Yūichi ought to have been tired from the long journey, but he couldn't get to sleep. Tomoko, who was on the other side of Tamio, kept tossing and turning and sometimes, as if she had suddenly just remembered, would raise her head and smile at me.

Holding my breath, I listened intently to the whistling sound of the powerful wind as it came sweeping from the Sea of Japan and seeped through cracks between the shutters. Eventually, I became aware that the waves didn't surge at equal intervals; their strength was different each time, as was the way they would swell. "It must be because of the wind. I wonder what the wind will be like in the winter." With these thoughts I closed my eyes and was just starting to doze off when Tamio's hand slipped under my quilt.

Each time the shutters rattled, I opened my eyes and stared at the miniature light bulb on the ceiling, wondering what the human heart really was. Surrounded by quilts and pillows permeated by someone else's scents to which I could never become accustomed, I moved my body naturally to receive him, just as I had done so many times before for you. But just that once, I tucked away in the back of my mind the image of you retreating down those tracks. I broke out in a sweat as the wind and waves roared.

THE DAYS THAT FOLLOWED were busy, but I felt that I belonged. Tamio was good to me. Since he was in charge of the young live-in chefs, on Sundays he would go to the inn at five o'clock in the morning to see to the guests' breakfasts, but unless there was a group tour, he didn't need to leave for work until ten in the morning on other days. Before a month passed, Tomoko was already comfortable calling me "Mom." My father-in-law really took to Yūichi, and every night after dinner would cradle him on his lap until he fell asleep. For his part, Yūichi saw Grandpa's lap as his exclusive spot, a place to go back to when he tired of playing. I became friendly with the neighborhood wives who passed me on the street wearing scarves over their bronze skin and carrying bamboo baskets on their backs. Sometimes I rode the bus with them to the morning market in Wajima.

My surroundings—the roar of the sea, the sound of the wind, the expansive view of the rough waves, the forlorn shaking of the leaves on the low Mount Ishiguro behind us, the desolate appearance of the scattered houses—soon felt less alien to me. And I got so that I was no longer surprised by the huge flocks of crows, gulls, and sparrows that would well up like billowing smoke or even by the large rainbows that would always appear over the horizon when the rain lifted. Once I settled in, the area on the tip of the Noto Peninsula seemed more poverty-stricken than I had imagined.

I realized how cheerless it was not to see young men and women in the prime of their working lives. The husbands of many of the women have gone to Tokyo for work and haven't been back since. Some of them disappeared without a trace and have sent no money for as long as five years. Their sons and daughters head to the cities to find work as soon as they graduate, start families, and never come back. Especially in Sosogi and the surrounding area, the fishing industry has been abandoned, and the village is full of elderly people and children. And yet owing to the boom in tourism over the past several years, during the travel season hotels and inns have more business than they can accommodate, and all over the tip of the peninsula people have been setting up bed-and-breakfast lodgings. It seems that students and office workers from the cities prefer a bed and breakfast over a large hotel or inn, and many of the families in the neighborhood have had their bath and toilet facilities remodeled and have hung out signboards from the Bed and Breakfast Association.

It was around the end of autumn that Tamio suggested that we follow suit. He broached the subject with hesitation, mentioning that he had wanted to do it for a long time, but since there wasn't a woman in the house. . . .

"Another drawback is that I'm working at an inn, and it would be like running a competing business on the side." But he had sounded out his boss at the inn and surprisingly found him to be fully supportive of the plan. His boss pointed out that inns and homes offering beds and breakfast attracted different guests anyway. And besides, when they were unable to accommodate people who showed up suddenly without a reservation, it would be to their advantage if they could keep the customers happy by referring them somewhere reliable.

"It was hard for me to bring this up, because it makes it seems as if I had you come here just for that. You'd end up doing most of the work." Tamio's apologetic explanation was that there was greater security in his working in the kitchen at the inn than in borrowing money to set up a second-rate eatery, but when the kids got older, his income from the inn might not be enough. He was of the opinion that, whatever life had in store for Tomoko, since Yūichi was a boy, he would like to send him to a top school. Aside from families having businesses in downtown Wajima, people were rarely able to send sons to college. I was grateful for Tamio's feelings. And besides, I enjoyed keeping busy with work, so we agreed that we would aim for the peak of the vacation season next year and work on home improvements gradually.

My first winter in Sosogi consisted of day after day of indescribable snow, wind, and rough waves. Listening to my father-in-law reminisce as we sat in the *kotatsu*, I realized just how resourceful and patient the people here at the tip of the Noto Peninsula had to be in order to survive in a place withered by briny winds, where they had no choice but to risk their lives by venturing out into the sea.

Wearing something Tamio said his grandmother had woven, a sort of thermal coat known in these parts as a *sakkori*, Yūichi played in the shallow snow. His cheeks were soon red and swollen from the cold, salty winds and caked with cracked mucous that he rubbed from his nose. It was comforting to see that his eyes, which had constantly shifted about restlessly when we lived in Amagasaki, now had a gentle calmness about them. I was glad that I had remarried. With some exaggeration, I told Mom in my monthly letter to her about my happy life in the Sekiguchi household.

Even so, when I heard Tamio and Yūichi laughing together in the bathtub as Tomoko and I were putting things away in the kitchen, I thought how delightful it would be if it were you in the tub with your son. Such thoughts would always send a chill down my spine, and I would be struck by an unsettling horror. It was not a horror at having such thoughts, but rather of you, who suddenly left this world. Why did you die? Why did you keep walking intently down the middle of the tracks until the moment you were hit? Where did you want to go by doing that? I paused with the dishes in my hands and, staring at a corner of the sink, began a frantic attempt to understand what goes on in the mind of someone intent on dying.

That day—about ten days into the New Year—the wind was especially fierce. In order to submit the documents for the bed and breakfast to the Public Health Center, I left Yūichi with his grandfather and boarded the bus to Wajima. I set out in driving snow, but when I finished my business and came out of the center, the storm had subsided. For the first time in a long time, I looked around in a large dress shop and went into a cosmetics store, where I made some small purchases. I walked toward Wajima Station along the narrow bus route lined with long-established lacquerware shops and had a cup of coffee at a coffee shop while waiting for the bus.

A man about thirty came in and ordered a cup of coffee. I could tell at a glance that he wasn't from around here. But he didn't look like a tourist either. He left the coffee shop without so much as taking a sip from the cup placed in front of him. What caught my attention was that he was terribly cross-eyed. His eyes looked like yours that night you stole the bicycle, when the more you rubbed your eye, the more it pulled to the side.

The man got on the same bus headed for Sosogi. Buses with tire chains move more slowly, and more than an hour went by before we passed through Ōkawa. The man, whose unoiled hair was neatly arranged, kept his weary gaze on the sea. Every time we came to a bus stop, he would begin to get up as if unsure whether or not to get off but would then sink back into his seat. Perhaps because of my sentimentalism I sensed something unusual about him. It occurred to me that he had come here to die.

The man got off at Kawara, one stop before Sosogi. When he got off, I could feel him look at me with his crossed eyes. I hurriedly got off the bus too and followed him without any thought of what I would do. Even though he had gotten off one stop before, he headed toward Sosogi along the frozen path beside the sea.

The crude houses facing the sea were all surrounded by rough-woven fences of sharp-tipped bamboo for protection from the wind and the spray of the waves. In a gust from the sea, snow packed like ice on the fence would fly off with a cracking sound. Spray from the waves pounding the breakwater rained down on my head. Snow whirled up from the roof tiles and was blown off toward the mountain. There was no one on the path but the man and me. My hands in their knitted gloves clutched the muffler wrapped around my head. I became soaked as I continued to follow him. Then the darkened sky and sea, the spray of the waves, the roar of the surf, the icy snowflakes all vanished, and I was walking with you along the rain-drenched rails late at night. You were walking away with your back to me and would not respond no matter how hard I clung to you. You wouldn't turn and face me no matter what I said. Nor would you have responded even to the pleas of the one who shared our blood. Ah, you just wanted to die. You didn't have any reason; you just wanted to die. The moment that occurred to me, I stopped following and stood motionlessly. You quickly receded from sight.

When I came to my senses, I was by a sand dune where a fishing boat, the *Matsumoto Maru*, had been abandoned. From a gap in the breakwater, I had gone down to the beach and up to the small white fishing boat, bending forward to make my way through the gusts from the Sea of Japan. Leaning against the boat, I watched the pitch-black sea come surging toward me. Both my muffler and my coat seemed as if they were about to be torn off by the wind. I felt neither cold nor fear. For a long time, I watched the winter sea, as if glued to the abandoned boat. My body was swaying along with the undulating sea. I wanted to go back to the tunnel tenement in Amagasaki. I didn't care any longer what happened. I didn't crave happiness. I didn't care if I died. Such thoughts filled my mind, accompanied by the crashing of huge waves. I wailed loudly, like a child. At that moment, it hit home to me with clarity that you had died. What a lonely, pitiable person you had been! I cried and cried, my face distorted with tears and sobs. I wonder how long I was there crying. Suddenly I looked to the side and saw Tamio standing there. I shrieked and for a while said nothing as I met his penetrating gaze.

"What's the matter? What are you doing in a place like this?" When I stepped away from him, he grabbed my shoulders and said, "Let's get into the house. You'll die if you stay here."

My father-in-law and Yūichi were asleep in the *kotatsu*. Tomoko was apparently at a friend's house playing and was nowhere to be seen. Tamio held my shivering body in his arms and led me upstairs, where he turned on the *kotatsu* and lit the kerosene stove. My mouth was numb; even if I had tried to talk, it wouldn't have been intelligible. I changed my clothes and curled up inside the *kotatsu*. The shivering wouldn't stop. Until I felt more like myself again, Tamio asked no questions. He poured me some hot tea, and when I finished drinking it, with a sharp look in his eyes he demanded that I tell him what was wrong. I said nothing.

"Do you dislike this family?" He asked in a gentle tone. I shook my head but had no idea how to explain.

"Looking out over the sea somehow made me depressed." When I finally spoke, the penetrating look in Tamio's eyes assumed a sternness that I had never seen before. "I was cold and sad, and somehow I just started crying."

"Why were you hiding in a place like that looking at the sea?"

Why had I blurted out that explanation then? Tamio and I glared at each other for a while, and then, in a coquettish whisper that surprised even me, I asked, "Which do you like more, your first wife or me?" There was a glimmer of relief in Tamio's eyes, and for the first time since our marriage, he made rough advances to me. I wanted to ask him how he had found me hiding on the other side of that fishing boat, but I just stared in silence at the texture of the discolored tatami.

THE HARSH WINTER CAME to an end, spring passed in an instant, and we opened our bed and breakfast establishment around the beginning of May, before the tourist season came into full swing. Our first guests were three students from Osaka. From then on, we were busy without a letup through the peak of the vacation season. We had only planned to do business during the summer and felt unprepared to handle guests who showed up in other seasons, their business welcome and at the same time a nuisance. When we were prepared for guests, our entire family would sleep in the ten-mat room downstairs, but when they showed up unexpectedly, we would have to scramble to put the upstairs in order. Since I had to provide guests with meals commensurate with what they had paid, I would sometimes have Tamio secretly deliver fish. Summer finally arrived, and we had guests continually through mid-September. The first year's guests recommended us to others, and the following year we had so many guests that at times our family had nowhere to sleep. After a year or two, we had assembled all the necessary utensils and bedding, and I had acquired a knack for managing the business and was able to calculate in an instant what would yield a profit.

Last fall I took Tomoko and Yūichi and returned to Amaga-saki for the first time in two years to attend the wedding of my brother, Kenji. Tamio had planned to go with us but decided that he simply couldn't leave his father alone like that.

"Your regular letters have put my mind at ease. Yūichi, you start school next year? You've really gotten to be a big boy." Mom had a room in the condominium that Kenji had recently moved into and appeared to be living comfortably.

"Kenji's business must really be doing well if he's able to afford a condominium with this many rooms."

"His wife teaches piano and has thirty students. She makes more than he does." Pointing at the large piano in the room, Mom gave a somewhat disgruntled laugh. "You should try listening all day long to the kids' awful playing. It's enough to drive you crazy."

I felt gratitude toward Kenji's wife, who was willing to live with Mom.

"They'd been living together for a month before the wedding. Young people these days don't care much about the order things are done in. But it seems I don't have to worry about you anymore."

"That's right, you don't."

Mom seemed pleased. She stroked Tomoko's face and said over and over with a smile, "I'm your grandma. And you're my granddaughter."

The next day, after the wedding, I went to see the tunnel tenement. It had been there when I left Amagasaki two-and-a-half years before but since then had been torn down and turned into a parking lot. After paying my respects to the former landlord couple who had arranged my match with Tamio, I went with Yūichi and Tomoko to a coffee shop near the park. It was good to see a place you used to go to occasionally, one that had not changed a bit. The young proprietor with curly permed hair was surprised to see me and came over to where I was sitting. He knew that I had remarried, and started reminiscing about you.

"It was about eight o'clock that day. He stopped by here and had a cup of coffee."

"That day?"

"Uh, the day he died. He'd finished work and stopped by for a cup of coffee on his way home."

"Oh."

"There wasn't anything particularly unusual about him, so it floored me when I read about it in the newspaper the next day. After all, he had sat at the counter and grinned as he listened to our idiotic banter."

"He stopped by here on his way home?" I asked vacantly. It would never have occurred to me that you had stopped by here, so close to home, and had coffee that night.

"He said that he'd forgotten to bring any money with him and that he would go right home and come back with it. I told him that next time he stopped by would be fine."

"Then he still owed you for the coffee?"

"He said, 'Sorry about that. I'll bring it next time, so thanks for the loan.' Then he went and committed suicide that night, so what he said somehow seems like a dream."

When I tried to repay the money you had borrowed, the proprietor declined with a wave of his hand. "No, that isn't why I mentioned it. I'm not trying to get the money back. No, no, I absolutely won't accept it."

On the train back to Sosogi, I kept thinking about the route you took that night to the very neighborhood where we had lived and from there to the middle of the train tracks. When you left the coffee shop, you weren't thinking about dying. I had no proof of that, but I was strangely convinced that it was so.

Then, what had happened to you after you left the coffee shop? I imagined it from as many angles as came to mind, considering various reasons why a person would resolve to die. And yet, I was unable to connect any of them with you.

I had never thought about the course of action you had followed that night. But I was only fooling myself to suppose that my thoughts came any closer to what had actually happened. Instead the two hours between then and your walking down the middle of the rails kept expanding into a vast, shapeless emptiness.

The first snowfall that year came on the third of December, starting in the middle of the night and stopping at daybreak. I awoke suddenly and looked at the clock by my bedside: a little past six. If it were spring or summer, the noises of people setting out in small boats to fish would be coming from the back door and from the beach, but after November there was never a sound. But that day I could hear the slow steps of someone along the side of the house, headed for the sea. It was the crunching sound of walking in deep snow. I thought, half awake, that it must have been heavy for a first snow. Not even the surf or the north wind was audible, and it almost made me wonder where I was.

I got up, lit the kerosene heater, put on Tamio's cardigan, and opened the shutters. A tranquil sunrise one wouldn't expect in the dead of winter had cast its glow over the sea, which was as silent as a swamp. The virgin snow, dyed by the sun's first rays, was such a bright red that it looked as if glowing charcoal embers had been spread evenly over the earth, covering roads, roof tiles, breakwaters, and beaches.

The footsteps were those of Mrs. Tomeno. She was a middle-aged woman who lived down a narrow path from the highway to Ushitsu, in a godown with wall tiles in a fish-scale pattern. Her husband had just recently set out for seasonal labor in Osaka. They raised barely enough rice for themselves on a small paddy. Sometimes, when the wind was calm, she would venture out onto the sea in a small engine-driven boat and make extra money selling her catch of perch and gilthead.

It occurred to me that, since Mrs. Tomeno was going out fishing, it must really be windless over the sea. She was cautious and would never take the boat out on a day when there was any danger of rough waves. What's more, she could predict the day's weather based on the wind and snow conditions so accurately that even the village elders would defer to her.

There is a small embankment of sand where the Machino River flows into the sea, and it was there that Mrs. Tomeno kept her boat. Wearing as many layers of clothing as possible, she was framed in the bright red of the morning glow as she walked along the snow-covered beach, emerging like some kind of divine figure. Mindless of the piercing, cold air, I watched her with fascination.

Noticing that I was watching from behind the shutters, she stopped and shouted something. When I made an inquiring gesture to indicate that I couldn't hear, she repeated, "I'm going out to fish for crabs. Won't you buy some?"

I knew that she would sell them at a reasonable price, so I nodded in response and held up three fingers.

"Three? Okay, I'll have three for you."

By then I was fully awake as I stood watching Mrs. Tomeno's boat move off into the sea, its engine buzzing. The sun was rising, and out over the sea, whose redness was suddenly fading, something glistening appeared. It spread out over a larger area than usual and began blinking. Whitecaps were nowhere to be seen. A light like golden powder was floating in the middle of the windless, silent sea. Mrs. Tomeno's boat finally became one with that light.

"Hey, shut the window! We'll have icicles inside the house."

At Tamio's protest, I closed the shutters and got back in bed.

"A lot of snow has fallen."

"Were you having secret conversations again with somebody while you were looking at the snow?"

I was taken aback, and asked, "Who do you mean by 'somebody'?"

Tamio rolled over in bed, twisted his body to face me, and said with a smile, "How should I know?" For a long time, he fixed his sleepy eyes on me. A glow appeared in his vacant, unblinking eyes. He slipped his hand toward me under the quilts and into my nightgown, and began groping me. Caressing my buttocks, he whispered, "I found them."

— 148 —

"What did you find?"

"There are freckles here, too. You have a butt like a teen-ager."

"Liar! There aren't any freckles there."

"It's true. Didn't you know?"

"No, I've never noticed anything like that."

It seemed that he was going to start groping again, so I pushed his hand away and stood up.

"Ever since I was kid, I've had a habit of sometimes talking to myself. Mom often got after me about it."

"I never have any idea what you're thinking. As the proverb says, 'A fair complexion hides seven calamities.'"

Just as I was brushing aside Tamio, who was persistent in his efforts to pull me toward him, the shutters began to rattle.

As I was preparing breakfast, too, the winds grew stronger, and the usual roar of the sea pressed in on us thunderously. The snow on the beach was whipped up and, like sheets of thin paper, flew off toward the village.

I was worried about Mrs. Tomeno, and from the small kitchen window surveyed the sea over which visibility was already limited to about twenty or thirty meters. Innumerable caps of waves were drawn toward the thick leaden sky in small waterspouts. The sea that had been so calm had changed with incredible suddenness.

Seeing that I was worried, my father-in-law said, "Every-thing's alright. Mrs. Tomeno is immortal, I tell you. She'll make it back even if she has to swim." But his usual smile disappeared from his face as he spoke. On his way to work, Tamio stopped by the office of the Fishermen's Union and reported that Mrs. Tomeno had gone out in a small boat to fish for crabs. The old men who were gathered there looked at each other, and then all spoke at once. "In this kind of weather, there's nothing we can do." All we could do was wait until the storm subsided.

By evening, the storm had still not abated. I recalled that morning's daybreak, so tranquil that you'd never think it was over the sea at Sosogi, and pictured Mrs. Tomeno's boat disappearing in a speck of light. The snow that had covered the beach had been swept away by the wind; the remaining patches had been frozen by the wild spray and looked like grey veins stretched over the earth.

It was then that the bus from Ōtani bound for Wajima stopped and Mrs. Tomeno got off. As if in a dream I raced out front. I made certain that my eyes were not deceiving me then ran to the office of the Fishermen's Union.

Mrs. Tomeno was surprised to find herself surrounded by so many old-timers, and for a while was unable to think of anything to say.

"I went out into the open sea, but it was too calm, and it started to give me the creeps. It hit me all at once that something was sure to happen. So before any signs of a storm appeared I hurried up and started back. I was just about fooled by the weather. I caught on right away, but even so I only had enough time to get the boat to the rocks at Maura Bay. I went from there to a relative's house, where I rested. Then I caught the bus that had been waiting for the storm to die down."

"That's our Tomeno! The sea can't hide anything from you." The old-timers were unanimous in praising and teasing her. As soon as she saw me, she held up a plastic bag and said with a nonchalant air, "Here's your share." At a loss for words, I took the three crabs, ran out of the saké-reeking office and made my way home against a blustering wind mixed with snow.

I realized that I had not paid for the crabs and went to Mrs. Tomeno's house after supper. Every step on the snowy path produced a sound like shattering glass. Light was filtering through the small window of the godown, which was surrounded by strings of persimmons and daikon hung out to dry. When I knocked on the door, Mrs. Tomeno called out in a loud voice, "Who is it? The door's open."

I handed her the money and was about to leave. She thanked me, saying that I needn't have come in the cold just for that, and offered me a cup of hot water.

"How did your first husband die?"

I had been asked that question by many people and each time had answered with whatever came to mind. But when Mrs. Tomeno asked in her abrupt, loud voice, I responded reflexively in kind, "Suicide. He was run over by a train."

"Oh my, that must have been hard for you."

For a while, Mrs. Tomeno was lost in thought. Her angled brows, together with the slant of her eyes, formed a thick-set diamond shape in the middle of her face. It was hard to determine whether her face concealed kindness or perverseness.

"I felt sorry for Tamio, too, when he lost Yoshie to an illness. She grew up in a temple not far from here. Tamio had planned to stay in Osaka, but he came back to Sosogi to marry Yoshie. He was really in love with her, so it must have been hard for him when she died so young."

After I got home, I took a bath with Yūichi and Tomoko. What was this about being "really in love with her," I wondered. After losing a wife he loved so much, why did he marry a woman like me?

"Do I have freckles on my bottom?" As I got out of the tub, I turned my buttocks toward Tomoko. She looked for a moment and then, pinching the area right above my crack, proclaimed, "Yes. Lots of them, right here."

Then she brought two mirrors and tried positioning them at different angles to show me. But the mirrors clouded up immediately, and I couldn't see anything.

"That's strange. They weren't there before."

Then Tomoko compared the freckles under my eyes and those on my buttocks again and again and kidded me saying, "Mom, the ones on your bottom aren't freckles. They're age spots." I laughed, suddenly recalling Tomoko's face the day I had arrived in Wajima, when she dipped her head and said, "Thanks for coming."

I got out of the tub and was toweling Yūichi when Tomoko got back in. She began to pester me to buy her this and that, all to be kept secret from her father. When she realized that I was in a bad mood, she stopped abruptly and tried to sneak away. "Get right in bed after you've dried you hair." I slapped her on the back.

That night, Tamio came home late and drunk. The storm had subsided, but the wintry coast of Sosogi was still assaulted by snowy wind and waves. To people who lived right by it, the deafening roar of the sea was no longer a sound at all. I have become so accustomed to it that it's just background noise now and it doesn't disturb my sleep.

"It's dangerous to drive when you've had so much to drink."

Tamio ignored me and curled up in bed without undressing. As I shook him, Mrs. Tomeno's "he was really in love with her" came to my mind and stuck there perversely. I was no longer able to suppress my jealousy of his dead wife. Throwing the quilt off him, I made him sit up, and screamed "Liar!" When a woman is beside herself with rage, she can't describe her own feelings. "You said that you came back to Sosogi against your will because you couldn't leave your father alone, didn't you?"

"Uh, yeah."

"I heard all about it. You came back from Osaka because you wanted to marry your first wife. I hear you were really in love with her. Why did you take up with a woman like me after losing such a precious wife?"

Tamio remained silent with a vacant look on his face, which threw me into an even greater rage, and I said without thinking, "Who do you think I'm always having private conversations with?"

"Who?"

"With you, with Tomoko, and with your father." Then, as if to cover my lie, I said, "I've done everything I can to become part of this family. Everything. I've thought and talked to my-self about it. But you, you came back to Sosogi just to marry the woman you were really in love with. You're a liar! You de-ceived me!"

I was screaming incoherently. Tamio chuckled and, as if humoring a baby, whispered, "Alright. Let's talk about it to-morrow. Okay? Let's save such terrible talk for tomorrow." Then he pulled the quilt over his head. But perhaps my silence made him uneasy, and he asked from under the quilt, "What's wrong? Are you asleep?"

At that moment, words I had never once spoken before slipped out. "When I start wondering why he committed sui-cide—why he was walking along the rails like that—I can't sleep any. Why do you think he did it?"

Tamio was silent. With his face buried in the quilt, I couldn't see his expression. I changed into my nightgown and got into bed. After a long time, when I had almost forgotten that I had posed the question, Tamio said, as if in reverie, "Maybe people want to die when they lose spirit."

"Spirit?"

His face finally emerged from under the quilt, and his breathing took on the rhythm of sleep. I closed my eyes and listened to the three of them breathe. My thoughts turned to the long time that had passed, from the tunnel tenement to the fishing village of Sosogi. My sorrow at having lost you is so out of the ordinary that it makes me shudder and has continued to haunt me with no end in sight. I lost a loved one through a suicide whose motives are beyond anyone's conjecture, one for which no reason can be found. Maddening vexation and grief lay coiled up within my breast, and because of that vexation and grief I have survived to this day. Tamio and Tomoko have become indispensable people to me, although I made no par-ticular effort or laid any plan to that end. And both Yūichi and I have become part of the Sekiguchi family. Perhaps talking to your retreating image has sustained me when I was about to wither away.

Your retreating figure alternately appeared and disappeared. That night as I lay there thinking, it was impressed in my mind what unhappiness really is. "Ah, so this is what it means to be unhappy." Such was my clear impression as I watched your retreating figure.

Before I knew it I dozed off, feeling as if I were floating on a warm sea. It was the same strange sense of relief I had experienced more than twenty years before when the police inspected under the floorboards and I lay with my head pillowed in Mom's lap. Both the roar of the raging sea and the violent rattling of the shutters pushed your retreating figure, tottering along the rain-drenched rails, further and further away, and I lay in deep relief.

WINTER PASSED AND SPRING arrived. Yūichi started elementary school.

I don't know what Tamio was thinking when he said it, and I haven't tried to find out, but I have come to believe that there is indeed an illness that robs people of their spirit—not something external like physical strength or mental vigor but an internal energy.

And perhaps, in the mind of someone afflicted with that illness, the momentary wavelets on the sea here at Sosogi would appear indescribably beautiful. Spring is at its height, and I became entranced gazing out over the deep green sea as it grew rough, then calm.

Look, it has started to glisten again! Depending on the conditions under which wind and sun mix, part of the sea will suddenly start to glisten like that. Perhaps that night, beyond the rails, you were looking at a similar light.

When I stare at it intently, it seems as if I can hear a pleasant sound accompanying the light of the waves. That one area is no longer the sea but more like a gentle, tranquil place not of this world, and I am drawn toward it. Yet anyone who has once seen the reality of the raging sea at Sosogi surely realizes that those wavelets are the entrance to the depths of a cold, dark sea.

Ah, it really feels good to talk to you this way. Sometimes, when I start talking, somewhere in my body a warm, pleasant ache wells up.

I can hear my father-in-law's phlegmy cough. When he's hungry and I'm loafing upstairs, that cough gets my attention. I wonder what he's recalling as he sits smiling on the veranda, day in and day out.

It's about time for Yūichi to get home from school.

About the Author

Miyamoto Teru (宮本 輝) was born in Kobe, Japan in 1947, and graduated from Otemon Gakuin University. He is a one of Japan's most popular writers, and becoming a globally acclaimed author with translations into multiple languages. His *Kinshu: Autumn Brocade*, also translated by Roger Thomas, was published in English translation in 2005.

Miyamoto's work reveals his consummate skill in creating such narratives with his sketches drawn from the working-class world of the Osaka-Kobe region in which he grew up, creating tales interspersed with vignettes informed by his own life experiences. He has earned a devoted following among the Japanese readership, and numerous awards including the Akutagawa Prize for *Firefly River* (蛍川).

About the Translator

Roger K. Thomas is a professor at Illinois State University where he teaches courses in East Asian languages and cultures and directs the program in East Asian Studies. His primary area of research is early modern poetics and kokugaku. He also has an active interest in modern fiction, his published translations including Miyamoto's *Kinshu: Autumn Brocade.*